THE CRIPPLE
AND HIS
TALISMANS

ANOSH IRANI

THE CRIPPLE
AND HIS
TALISMANS

ALGONQUIN BOOKS OF CHAPEL HILL

2005

Published by
ALGONQUIN BOOKS OF CHAPEL HILL
Post Office Box 2225
Chapel Hill, North Carolina 27515-2225

a division of
Workman Publishing
708 Broadway
New York, New York 10003

This is a work of fiction. While, as in all fiction, the literary perceptions and insights are based on experience, all names, characters, places, and incidents are either products of the author's imagination or are used fictitiously. No reference to any real person is intended or should be inferred.

Library of Congress Cataloging-in-Publication Data
Irani, Anosh, 1974–
    The cripple and his talismans / Anosh Irani.—1st ed.
        p. cm.
    ISBN-13: 978-1-56512-456-1
    ISBN-10: 1-56512-456-1
    1. Bombay (India)—Fiction.   2. Suffering—Fiction.
    3. Amputees—Fiction.   I. Title.
PR9199.4.I73C75 2005
813'.6—dc22   2004062388

10 9 8 7 6 5 4 3 2 1
First Edition

03043 1330

For my grandparents,
Perin and Burjor Motiwala.

CONTENTS

PROLOGUE

In the beginning there was a little boy. He was alone in the universe and everything was dark and quiet.

One day he saw a tree, very far away. Then it vanished and everything was dark again. Being simple and humble by nature, the boy became scared and wished for strength. In his heart he felt warm; the warmth spread all over his being.

"What did my vision mean?" the boy asked. He waited for an answer, but none came.

"I must make the place of the tree like its many limbs," he decided. "Let them branch out to become the roads of the world. Let none of them ever be cut off."

He made the place and its tree out of the distance, and waited for a long time. He observed this place during his wait, and was not happy with what he saw. So he flew to it.

There he saw another forked form that he had created. It was like a walking tree, and he called it Man. Man was bent over, entangled in his own embrace.

"You use your limbs wrongly," said the boy. "They are meant to embrace others, not yourself."

The boy freed Man of his own clasp. "Now use your limbs well," he said.

The boy saw another form and named it Woman. He realized that there were many forms gathered there. He named them all: Tiger, Snake, Smoke, Tree, Fire, Soil, Water and Wind. The boy flew above them all because he could.

"This is the place of the tree with its many limbs," he told the forms. "You must use them well, and let none of them be cut off."

All the forms were confused.

"These limbs branch out to become the roads of the world," the boy explained.

Smoke was still unclear.

"In life, there are three main paths," the boy explained again. "The first one is crooked. It means that you are simply pretending to come toward me. Only the sly and devious shall take this path."

Hearing this, Snake slithered away, dragging Soil with it. Tree needed Soil to live, so it followed.

"Next is the straight path. It leads only to me. It is very long and few will complete it. There is nothing to do along the way, except pray."

In truth, the road that led to the boy was the most wondrous of all roads. But the boy had no wish to present it as such. This was a test. But none of the forms took that road.

"The third path has the possibility of flying, of tigers, of flying tigers," said the boy. "It means anything can happen."

It was Woman who first walked on the third path. She needed things to make her happy. So she took Tiger to ride on, Fire to keep warm, Water to wash her hair and Wind to blow through it. Smoke followed because Fire went.

The boy was upset with these choices. By not taking the straight path, the forms had cut off a limb. Only Man was left, so the boy turned to him.

"Go away," said Man. He motioned the boy away with a flick of the wrists. And once again Man was entangled in his own embrace.

The boy told him, "I can see what is going to happen here. There will be magic, poverty, thievery, music, pollution, dancing, murder, lust and very little prayer."

"Leave me alone," said Man. "Promise me that you will never come here again."

"First tell me what this place is called," said the boy, "so I remember never to visit it, for it is no longer the place of the tree."

"Bombay," said Man. "There is no other like it."

"Thank God," said the boy.

It was then that the boy realized who he truly was. He kept his promise never to return.

THE IN-CHARGE

The man's look tells me that I have made a mistake. He moves closer to my face, but his eyes focus on the dim light bulb that hangs above me in the center of his beedi shop. His skin is soot, dark but smooth. Mosquitoes are converging around the bulb. He listens to their murmur.

"Yes, I'm the In-charge," he whispers.

He looks at the mosquitoes around the bulb. They stick to it and exchange places with one another, a small dance to pass time between transmissions of malaria.

I try to get his attention. "Gura has sent me," I tell him. "He says you have information about my lost arm."

He covers my mouth. His palm smells of tobacco and money. There is also the stink of genitals but I try to dismiss that. He releases his hand slowly.

"I will draw a map for you," he says.

It is dim and dusty, and I am being hit and bitten by insects. I realize that he waits for me to respond.

"A map will be helpful," I say.

His dark hands are beautiful compared to the rest of him. His face is round as an earthen pot and his ears are long. Strands of hair with the dryness of straw stick out of his lobes. But his hands are thin as if crafted from black paper. Mine are lighter, more the color of soil. I am one hand less now; in fact, a whole left arm less, if one insists on staring at me under the mosquito bulb.

He plucks out a short pencil from behind his ear. Apart from Shivaji beedis, he also stocks packs of Marlboro, Gold Flake, Charminar, Dunhill, Four Square and 555 on thin wooden shelves. I look at his small shop and wonder how he stays in this hole all day. I look to the side, at the shop next to his. It is a flower shop, just as constricting. Most of the flowers are dead. White buckets hold the fragrant corpses.

He now has a piece of paper on top of the glass jar that contains sweets. The paper already has numbers scribbled all over it so I do not know how he will draw a map.

"You are here," he says, his eye on the paper.

He draws a spiral, keeps circling. In order to make him stop before he puts a hole through the paper, I respond. "I understand, In-charge."

I use his title in the hope that he will reveal his name.

"You are here," he repeats. The circling continues. "You must follow a few landmarks. They will direct you to the games. But I cannot tell you what the landmarks are."

"Games? What games?"

He hands me the chit of paper. One spiral shows me where I am. Two inches from it, a darker spiral shows me where I must go.

Let me have my arm for just a second so I can teach him a lesson. I am not accustomed to being mocked. I am a novice cripple.

"At least tell me which direction I must take," I ask the In-charge.

"You will know. I'm busy. Now go."

No one is around. If there were customers, I could understand if he said he is busy. But not even the flower man is visible. We are in one of the city's gullies, a by-lane that only the local residents use.

I take the map and walk out on the street. I hold it under the streetlight with my right hand. If I had both arms, I would have a better grip. I try not to think of my disability. At times it makes me so rabid that I want to rip my other arm off. I then realize that I do not have an arm to pull the other one off. This angers me even more.

A lost arm causes much more than physical disorientation. I question many more things. Why does so and so have an arm? Why is he happy? Why is she beautiful? Why is the orange that I eat sour?

I think of Gura the floating beggar. It was he who led me to the In-charge. The moment I lost my arm, two months ago, I felt like a pariah in the company of normal people. After I got out of the hospital, I sold my white-marbled apartment by the sea and moved to one with stone flooring, where flying cockroaches and mosquitoes sang at midnight. I did not speak a word for two whole months. It was as though my arm had done the talking before.

Gura was the first person I talked with, this very morning. It happened naturally. In my new physical state, I recognized Gura as my equal — a beggar I could speak to. Gura's remark startled me.

"Don't worry. You'll get used to it," he said.

He sat at the entrance to my building. I had never noticed him before. Was it obvious that I had recently lost an arm? I looked at him and saw the face of darkness — a little hell, fallen trees.

"What will I get used to?" I asked. These were the first words I had uttered in two months. Instead of feeling better, I felt as though I were choking on my own vomit.

"Absence," he said. His body and face were more stained than the footpath he sat on. "There is an absence," he continued. "And you are not handling it well."

Why should I? I thought. It is not as if I have lost my wallet. In fact, even when I lost my wallet I never handled things gracefully.

Then he leaned toward me. "Now listen," he whispered.

Gura scratched a boil on his thigh. He picked out flakes from his scalp. He bared his teeth to the sun until they got hot. He licked his lips, tweaked his eyebrows and crossed his arms.

"Why are you staring at my face?" he asked.

"You said to listen."

"Not to me."

"To whom, then?"

"The street. All answers lie in its sounds. In the bicycle bell of a little boy also lies the wail of his mother, for she knows he will leave her soon when he is crushed by a speeding truck."

"That's quite dark."

"*He* is dark."

"Who?"

"You tell me."

"Why are you talking in riddles?"

"How are riddles shaped?"

"I don't know."

"They coil round and round like gullies."

"Why are you telling me this?"

"You're sucking it out of me like a mosquito."

"No, I'm not."

"If there is a dispute then talk to the In-charge."

"Who?"

"The In-charge!"

Beggars do that, I thought. They feel God has abandoned them so they put someone else in charge. Poverty strips them of their brain. They start counting colors instead of money, and when colors run out they try and invent their own. That drives them to madness because it is impossible to think of a color that does not exist.

So I walked past Gura and up the four steps that led to my flat. I was about to open the door when he said something that made my heart pound.

"The In-charge knows about your lost arm. That which you do not."

Words like this come once in a lifetime, and you hear them even if your ears have been torn from your head and stamped into the earth.

"What does he know?"

"Ask him."

"Where can I find him?"

"Your arm will show you. Point it."

I raised the only arm I had toward the fire temple in the distance. Gura shook his head. I pointed to the post office and the three-star hotel. Then to the flyover and dancing bars below. The

Central and State Banks, the old Parsi library, the gas cylinder shop, the nursing home known for selling babies when mothers were not looking. Soon all of these had been indicated.

"I'm lost," I said.

"Then use your lost arm."

"But it does not exist."

"Nothing really does."

I faced the old cinema that showed B-grade Hindi movies. I imagined I was using my absent arm to point. Since I had time, I turned toward the clock repair shop. Then I pointed at the toy shop whose sad moustachioed owner looked like he was selling sick puppies instead. I had spun a complete 360 so I looked at Gura, who urged me to carry on.

"But I'll keep going round and round in circles," I said.

"Like a Jalebee!" he laughed.

I felt very foolish. A beggar was mocking me. So I reached into my shirt pocket and pulled out some money. It was the only way to save face. A rich man without an arm is still superior to a poor man with one.

"It's a hint," said Gura.

"You want to eat Jalebee?" The poor fellow suddenly had a craving for orange coiled sweets?

"You can't eat this Jalebee. But can you go to it."

I understood.

There was only one area in the city where gullies wound like riddles, where the in-roads were black as death, messages from prophets were scribbled on the walls and babies walked like tiny gangsters, toting guns and milk bottles.

"Jalebee Road?"

"Good work, my crippled genius."

"Will you take me there?"

"I have begging to do! You think I can afford to waste time?"

"Then how will I find the In-charge?"

"Even the blind can find him."

So when night fell, I walked to Jalebee Road. In the heart of Jalebee Road there is a tree. It is the oldest tree in the city, without leaves, and is considered holy, a refuge for all lost souls. It is said that a sage sits in its hollow, an addict who has run out of ganja, who heals the sick and poor by sucking the sadness out of their lungs. (No one has proved this, but people do feel better after circling the tree.)

So I went round and round the tree. After all, I was a lost soul, too — I did not know where to go. Even though there were a few people near the tree, they ignored me. Then an old woman, as bent as the tree itself, joined me. She walked as though it was a marriage ceremony and she was my ancient bride. Perhaps her husband had abandoned her on their wedding day many years ago. If it made her feel better, who was I to enlighten her? We both circled, but she soon wandered off toward the balloon factory in the distance. I must have circled the tree one hundred times.

I was so dizzy, the residents of Jalebee Road flew toward me.

The street children came first. They flew sideways and they were all scratching their heads and laughing. In their laughter I could hear the shouts of their fathers, too: drunk, angry at the walls, washing the dirt off their lips with every sip. Suddenly Gura's words made sense. All answers lie in the sounds of the streets.

So I closed my eyes and opened myself up to the sounds around me. The blaring horn of a truck said "move out of the way or I'll kill you"; the wind blew through the old, bare tree and made a wailing sound as it yearned for leaves. But it was the bark of a stray dog that made me open my eyes. It sounded like the cough of a wise old man who had walked down from the hills, past the plains and into this winding pit.

There was a deep gash in the dog's white skin. As it licked the flies off the wound, I saw its cold, silver eyes. The dog was blind. Yet it looked straight at me and smiled. Was it laughing at my deformity? Then it sniffed the earth, licked an ant-ridden packet of Glucose biscuits and walked past me toward a narrow lane. Just before it entered the lane, it turned around and spoke in garbled sounds, dog language, in which A's are yells, B's are cries, C's are pleas and D's are direct commands.

I heard a distinct D. Follow me, it said.

And then I understood Gura's final words. Even the blind can find the In-charge. A blind animal would lead me, if I was humble enough to allow it. It went past the cheap tailors and roadside barbers, and stopped outside a small cigarette shop. It was very dark and all I could see at the counter was a light bulb. It was so dim, it seemed to spread darkness around with confidence, as if it were a cure for light. Not a soul was around. The dog whimpered, raised its hind leg and watered the parched earth.

I leaned over the counter and saw a dark man, born of the night bulb itself, hiding in his own shop, speaking to his glass jars filled with sweets, whistling to his packets of supari and paan masala, counting money fast-fast. I asked him if he was the In-charge.

"Yes, I'm the In-charge," he finally whispered.

So now here I stand, late at night, in one of the by-lanes of

Jalebee Road, and stare at the map the In-charge has just given me. I hope it gives me some clue as to where I must go next. It can be north or south of the shop. You will know, the In-charge said.

I hear a sound, a cough.

A man is asleep on a handcart, a rag over his eyes to stop the streetlight from invading. Slowly he turns in his sleep. The rag of cloth is off his face. Maybe I should take my first bearings from him. His head is north, his feet south. One uses one's head to think, so maybe that is where I should head. But one uses feet to walk. So perhaps south is where I should walk.

The logic of the armless.

The man coughs again. I see his face clearly and another thought strikes me. The man looks South Indian. I shall go south.

As I walk, I wonder what I am doing here. I am sensible, literate. I should handle my loss with dignity.

I question the In-charge's actions. Why can't he just tell me where I must go? As I look behind me, the beedi shop is now the size of a sugar cube. Maybe I have walked far enough. I look at the map again. The first spiral is light. The second spiral, my destination, darker.

The human mind is weak. Scribbles on a chit of paper taunt it. I think about the fried eggs I had in the morning. Did I put too much pepper on them? Whenever I am reminded of my arm, I try to think of mundane things. This tactic is as useful as the map I hold.

The street gets darker. This is strange, since the streetlights are at an equal distance from each other and all of them work. With each step I take, darkness envelops me. I feel the tip of her fingers, the softness of her palm, the warmth of her hands against my face. I hear her hum — it is the sound of the universe and only I am meant to hear it, under a sky that is as black as the hands that touch me. Darkness prays for me, a prayer that will keep me in its womb for as long as I can remain. Even comfort gets hard to bear, she says. I believe her because a mother is to be believed. As she recedes, she glides down my arm and leaves. A mother has many children, she says. She must care for them all.

I have entered the darker spiral.

You will know, the In-charge said. The mosquitoes know. The man on the handcart knows. My feet know and they will take me there.

I take off my slippers and throw them to the side of the street. The soles of my feet are pleased to feel patches of dirt and soil. Open drains gush around me. Dirty water speaks underneath us all. I am certain the games are near.

I walk a little farther and I see three, maybe four, bodies come toward me. Their walk is slow and deliberate. I try to remain calm. They can take nothing from a cripple. To my left, I see three forms about fifty feet away, slightly thinner, shapely. Where are all these people coming from?

Two armored vehicles, the color of rust, glide to the center of the road and halt. I cannot see the drivers. Headlights burn the earth. On the ground, the outline of a large circle is drawn in white chalk. The human forms are closer and real. They converge on this center, which is being built around me. I can see the people now, and I know I have found the place.

The games have found me.

Of course the In-charge knew I would find the games. It was never in my hands to begin with. Some sort of army has decided to meet here. There are women with acid burns, their faces the road map to ancient ruins. Women I cannot look at because I know that only man can inflict such impairment. Their saris wound around them with preciseness, the women take protection in any form, even a thin layer of cloth. There are beggars, some on wooden platforms with wheels. The stumps of their feet shine in the headlights as if they have been oiled meticulously. Even stumps look different. God is a genius: no two arms look alike. Cut them off, and no two stumps are identical. What more proof does one require of God's creation?

I look at their faces and I am not surprised that I recognize some of them. It is not a mystery that all beggars look the same. They *are* the same, floating beggars. You see them at one traffic light, asking for money in God's name. You see them at another traffic light, pleading that one of their relatives is dead and money is needed for the funeral. You think: this beggar has a resemblance to the one seen in another part of the city, or at the previous signal. Clouds float, and when you look up from taxis, you can swear they follow you. Beggars do the same.

The floaters come to the edge of the circle. Wheels scrape on concrete. Blue sari-clad eunuchs are present, too. Most of them are man-made; all that was man in them was removed.

The armored trucks are still running. I am certain they contain valued goods.

Then, through the stream of acid women, I see the In-charge. He looks blacker here, in the face of headlights. There are at least fifty people now, representations of everything that is wrong with the world, everything that will remain unchanged because normal people are in charge. Here we all have one heartbeat, one drum that God beats, upon which he inflicts soulful migraines.

The In-charge raises his right arm. He wears a lungi and a white vest, and I notice that he is well fed. His hands might be thin and beautiful, but his stomach is a lewd protuberance.

The doors of the two armored trucks open. From each armored truck steps a human form that is hard to behold. I feel normal in their presence. These are not figments of an armless man's delirium. These are lepers. I try to remember the hum of darkness, thinking it will soothe me, but I cannot.

The only thing that differentiates the lepers is the cloth that covers them from lower belly to knee. One is black, the other white. Perhaps this is why I have been sent here, to feel better about myself. In the presence of the diminished, greatness can be achieved. Arm or no arm, I am now a giant.

The armored trucks make sense. If an ordinary vehicle were to transport these two, they might not make it here. They are so fragile, the wind might blow their fingers off. The engines shut off.

Silence.

We could have heard a bird chirp in another universe.

A sound: the scraping of feet.

The leper in black holds one leg and walks, assisting the leg itself with a hand that is wrapped in bandages. The other has a stronger walk but his face has receded more, itching to kiss skull. They walk to the center of the circle and face each other. I cannot see their eyes and I am glad. The In-charge positions himself between the two.

A little girl, no older than ten or eleven, with long black hair parted from the center into two neat plaits, runs to the lepers with two garlands in her hands. Faces with the geography of hell are treated to the scent of heaven. The lepers bend low to accept their garlands. They are humble.

"Sisters and brothers," shouts the In-charge. "To see so many good persons in one gathering warms me. Our custom will remain the same as always. We will start after our prayer."

Something touches my feet. I look down, and it is a beggar seated on the ground. He has no legs. He extends his arm. I do not know what to do. He takes my hand. I feel someone's palm on the stump of my left shoulder. It is a eunuch's. I look around and everyone is holding hands — acid women connected to eunuchs, eunuchs to amputees, amputees to beggars.

What are they all praying for? Their limbs to grow back? I tell myself that destiny exists; if not, what can explain my body being touched by these people?

Then the In-charge raises his arms, looks to the sky and closes his eyes. He chants, and I have never heard anything like it. It is the song of a dying man sending his last words to heaven, asking the ones who are already there to come receive him. Everyone joins in. Slowly the chants fade, as if large birds are transporting these sounds on their backs and carrying them far away from us.

I open my eyes only when I hear the shuffling of feet. The In-charge stares at his watch. "It's midnight," he says. "Let the games begin!"

He then lifts the little girl in his arms and joins the crowd.

The lepers walk to opposite sides of the circle.

The one in black screams. It is a summons to all the lepers of the city; in every sewer, under every bridge, beside every beedi shop, there is a leper who hears it and feels the juice of life in his sores.

The one in white does not move, but his fingers are curled into a fist. He waits for the other to come to him.

Now the two are only feet apart.

They are illuminated by the headlights.

The one in white strikes first; a blow to the face.

The crowd roars. A eunuch shouts to the skies: "Forgive them!" Forgive whom? For what?

The beggar beside me spits, whether in disgust or glee I cannot tell. He thumps his tin can to the floor repeatedly.

The one in white moves again. With great force he steps onto the other's foot. There is a deep hole in it, near the ankle. The outer rim of the hole is black, the inner rim is yellow and the core is white as ivory. With his heel still dug in, the leper in white thrusts his hands onto his opponent's chest, pushing him away. He lifts his foot and watches the leper in black fall to the floor. The sight is terrifying. Three toes lie on the concrete.

I look for the In-charge, for some signal to explain this horror, but he is not visible. I want to look away, but the only sound I hear is that of the beggar's tin can beating the concrete.

In the glare of the headlights I see the whites of the lepers' eyes. The vanquished one does not recover from the onslaught. He lies on the ground, as torn as the garland petals that lie by his feet. He looks to the sky. Is there a spirit world up there? Is there a separate one for lepers? Does the soul of a leper have leprosy?

At this moment I could donate the excess of blood in me to each hospital in the city, it pounds so hard, gushes so furiously. It could spurt from my mouth and make the city brighter.

I could make dying oxen dance.

The In-charge reappears. He raises both his arms. I wish I could raise mine. I have raised my arms in the past, but only to pull things down, curtains and people alike. It is sometimes more convenient to raze lives than raise them.

The In-charge walks to the center of the circle and goes to the lepers. No, he walks past them and comes toward me.

Do not come here. I do not wish to be singled out, a sparrow among lions.

An endless row of eyes stares at me.

It is easy to stand on a pulpit and lecture about how the world sits on a dog's tongue, that each time the dog licks excrement, it coats the world with a layer. That we are all bad people, and that we must be punished. I ask all holy men to stand here today. Wisdom will escape them like worms from fruit. They will feel naked and shake, and hope that their eyes do not meet a leper's.

"You must be part of the proceedings," the In-charge says.

"Please, I'm okay," I reply. I would give my other arm to be somewhere else.

"You must earn your right to be here."

"I don't understand." I say that to buy time.

"Come with me," orders the In-charge.

He holds my hand and takes me to where the leper in black is on the ground. The other leper looks on.

"Now help him up," the In-charge tells me.

"But he's a leper!"

"I'm aware of that."

"But if I touch him . . ."

"Help him."

"Why me?"

"You must earn the right to be here."

"No one told me that."

"Do it. Now."

I look around.

I extend my arm.

For the leper on the ground, it is a shaft of light.

He holds it with both hands. His hands are hot.

I lift him.

The crowd disperses. They turn and go on their way, to their brothels, their begging spaces and their drinking cells.

"Why is everyone going?" I ask.

"They are mere spectators. This is *your* moment."

"My moment?"

"It is why you have met me. Help this man here. He is the victor." He turns to the leper in black.

"But he lost," I say. "The one in white tore off his toes!"

"The winner is he who loses his ugly parts. The loser is he who is left with them."

The leper in black, the one who has been relieved of his rotting toes, looks surprised. The lepers must not have known the rules of the fight. They were tricked. And rightly so, or else they would have ripped off their own body parts.

"It's his turn to be free," says the In-charge.

"Free?" I ask.

"He has done his time. As his body slowly comes apart, he will be relieved of it. He will be cleansed soon."

The leper in black bows his head. The one in white snarls and walks away.

"What about him?" I point to the one in white. I am conscious of the manner in which we speak, as though the lepers are not part of our world.

"He gathered the festering parts, so he lost tonight. He's not ready. He must do more time."

"What does all this have to do with me?"

The In-charge whispers into the leper's ear. The leper then looks at me from the corners of his eyes. He turns slowly toward me. I hope he does not touch me.

The leper puts his hand in his mouth.

He bites hard onto his forefinger. He does so as though he is eating a dark biscuit.

Pthuck.

A snap, like that of a dry twig.

The finger stays in his mouth, caught between his teeth. If I give him a match, he might smoke it. He picks it out of his mouth.

"Take it," says the In-charge.

And dip it in my tea? Offer it to others as a vintage cigar?

"It's an offering," urges the In-charge.

"I'm okay," I say.

"The victor must relinquish his finger. One by one, he will renounce all his body parts until he ceases to exist. Only then will he be cleansed. You cannot let him down."

"But . . ."

"It's crucial that you take it."

"I . . ."

"Do it!"

"Can't he give it in a bag?"

"Listen, friend, do it for your own sake."

I extend my arm, a naughty child holding his hand out for the schoolmaster's cane.

"Is this how you accept an offering?"

I cup my hand.

The finger feels scaly. A dry piece of dog shit.

The leper taps the stump of my arm.

He comes close to my ear. His breath captures the essence of an entire hospital.

"Baba Rakhu," he whispers.

A THOUSAND OIL LAMPS

Not far from Jalebee Road is an old burnt-down mill by the sea. I stop to rest in its ruins. As I left the games, the cries of the lepers tried to pull me back. That is why it took me an hour to get here.

The mill resembles an ancient temple. I stand under a half-eaten archway. There are hubs in the walls, carved out for the gods. Under the moon the hubs hold light, tempting us to drink it. If only we could drink light.

Dark leaves move in the trees. I walk toward a slab of stone in the distance. On either side of me there is exposed brick. I hear the waves hit the shore. I want to sit by the sea and watch the small boats in the distance. Men are sea urchins at heart. We like being lost at sea, being rescued and given little huts to live in on the shore. But as time goes by, we lose ourselves in the water again. I take my place on the stone. It is cold. I stare into the night and wonder if the sea looks as widowed during the day.

I used to have an apartment by the sea. I never saw the sun rise because I was too busy drinking gold of my own the night before. When your head aches, you shut out the sound of waves; only the splashing of whiskey is heard, as your shaking hand raises the bottle to your mouth. I used to drink water, too. Water is a wonderful drink. It clears out the toxins to make way for more potent ones. Waves do the same. That is why they foam.

I think too much. I must shut down my brain and only see. But then I see too much. For example, right now a woman stands in front of me. I do not know where she has come from. She carries the glow of caves. Maybe she was born from the salt of the sea. I am surprised but not scared. After the leper fight, anything else is a song.

"Isn't it beautiful?" she asks.

I look down at the stone I sit on.

"Not the stone," she says. "I'm talking about the rainbow."

Ruins do that to people. They see strange things. They see lions in the moonlight, licking honey from the hands of a child.

"It's just come out," she says. She looks at the archway that I stood under only moments ago.

"You mean the archway is in the shape of a rainbow?"

"That's not an archway. It's a rainbow."

I do not argue, only make certain that I still have the leper's finger in my pocket. It has no use now, and maybe it never will. It is a fitting token for a man seeking the truth about his lost limb.

"I would like your help," she says.

Help is a cunning dog. It comes to you on all fours, and as you bend lower to pet it, scratches your eyes out.

"I have lost my family in the fire that burnt this mill," she says.

"I don't have any money," I tell her. In the distance I hear transport trucks. The strain on their engines tells me they are moving uphill.

"What will I do with money?" she says. "I'm already dead."

I do not ask her why she thinks she is dead. Maybe she means the loss of her loved ones has killed her soul.

"I sell rainbows," she says. "It's my job."

"Where do you get them?" I do not know what else to ask.

"I make them myself. When I have sold enough, I shall be free to return to my husband and son. Until then, I must live in these ruins."

"How much for one?" I ask. I get up from the stone and slap the dust off my legs.

"You don't understand," she says. "I must convince you that the archway is a rainbow. That will be considered a sale."

"But it is an archway," I protest.

"Exactly. That's what makes my job difficult."

When I had both my arms, the people I met were ordinary. They were perfectly formed, but ordinary. Ever since my loss, I have run into beasts who hold the meaning of the earth between their teeth.

"Please," she says. "I want to be with my family again."

I take a hard look at the archway. It is damp. "I see the rainbow," I tell her.

She shakes her head and looks to the ground. "No sale is that easy. Walk with me to where the boats sail."

I have walked this way many times before, holding a bottle, running my hands through my hair, catching the wind in my fist and sending it back to the sea. In the dark, I have used these walls to press against the insides of a woman's thighs. I have heard each wave come in to the shore and call their names in alphabetical order: Aarti, Damini, Gauri, Hema, Layla, Payal, Reshma, Roxanne,

Tarana, Zeenat. The tips of my fingers knew their hips better than the silk that once covered them.

From a distance, the small boats look as if they can be toppled over with a finger. Perhaps that is the meaning of my gift. I will stand on the shore and overturn boats with the leper's finger, send fishermen to the bottom of the sea.

"Look down," she says. "What do you see?"

There is sand and gravel. Large pieces of stone are visible, too. I assume they are the remnants of the mill. There are also bits of rusted broken glass.

"Do you see the sand?" she asks.

"Yes."

"What color is it?"

"Black."

"No, it's white."

I simply look at the boats; I know an explanation is not far away.

"The sand is always white. Only our eyes darken it. Look at it again."

"It's still white," I affirm.

"Correct."

"What?"

"It's still white," she smiles.

"I did not say that," I tell her.

"Your eyes have lightened the soil."

I look at the sand and gravel again. It is whatever I want it to be. It can change in a blink.

"I will light a thousand oil lamps for you," she says. "I will send them out to sea. You will need them to light the road before you."

She walks back to where the sand and gravel meet the mill walls. She is gone only a minute. She returns with a burning oil lamp cupped in her palms. It is a tiny earthen bowl filled with oil and a wick. The flame flickers gently in the breeze, almost dying out, then displaying the spark of a newborn. I must have heard her wrong. I thought she said she would light one thousand oil lamps.

She walks past me toward the water. She bends and carefully places the oil lamp on the water's surface as though she is parting with the ashes of a loved one. The oil lamp floats away and the flame gets stronger.

"A prayer has been lit," she says. "A special one for you."

In the past I have been told that I needed prayers, but no one bothered to say one for me. When I had two arms, I never joined them in prayer myself. It is said that the only form of light that travels upward from the earth is prayer.

"The flame will go out soon," I say. I doubt my purity. Anything lit for me will meet its dark fate sooner than a ship with a hole in its heart.

"It will go out only when your journey is complete."

"Who said I'm on a journey?"

"Look back at your starting point," she says. "You've already walked a long way."

I turn around and instantly recognize the archway. It looks beautiful in the night. It is red. It is yellow and blue. It is any color I want it to be.

"That's a rainbow," I say. "There's no doubt about it."

"How can you be so sure?" she asks.

"Can you prove it is not?"

"At last I can return to my husband and son," the woman says after a pause. "I did not know until this moment, but this was my final sale."

She looks at the sea with such longing, I am convinced she will walk into the water and never come back. "Remember this," she says. "A sworn enemy will try and end your journey before it is truly over."

"If that happens, what should I do?" I ask.

"Look for a rainbow," she says. "Now go home. An evil eye was cast upon you. You must stay there until you find a way to close it."

I look to the sea again. The oil lamp has given birth to many. An army of light sails toward the horizon. There are oil lamps everywhere, around the boats, on the crests of waves. Even the fish carry oil lamps on their backs. This is what God's skin must look like. Smooth water and light as far as the eye can see. I turn to my left to ask the woman if the ruins are causing my madness but she is gone.

There are at least one thousand oil lamps. They coast along to the next country, to the next world, to the mouth of God.

THE EVIL EYE

I live on the ground floor of a sinking building. Like most of the tenants here, the building is very old. Each day it sinks lower into the ground. I am not regarded fondly by its tenants. I have written an open letter to them all, proclaiming that I wish the entire building would go underground with all of us in it. It is the weight of our collective hearts that is pulling it down, but no one else believes this.

It is dawn. I have spent the rest of the night staring out the window. I am unable to eat. I tried to eat a carrot last night after I got home, but it turned into a human finger right before my eyes. So I decided to fry eggs. As I cracked open the first egg, I saw a tiny human baby inside, laughing at me. It leapt out of the egg and flew away into the night. After that I simply lost my appetite.

Dawn breaks. It breaks the poor first.

Get up, dip piece of bread in tea, shit outside, brush with fingers, leave fallen hair in dust, have gentle chat with neighbor about dying, live for nothing. No alms, no arms — we are all poor.

I was not aware of these delightful mornings before. I used to have breakfast in bed at 3 p.m. Toast and eggs, tea with honey. My honey's name would change according to whom I brought home the night before. Did you know that honey is never sweet in the morning? If you have forgotten its name, it will turn sour and poison your tea. I loved all kinds of honey, no matter which part of the country it came from. Now I wake up alone. Only the eggs remain.

Living alone affects me. I have no one to compare myself to. I know that most people have two arms, but there are other things. Does everyone have one eye smaller than the other? When you keep your hands still for too long, do they move on their own? Do brown flying cockroaches visit us all?

The tube lights in my kitchen seem extra long, longer than when I bought them at the electronics shop. Moths always collect around them, sticking to the hot light, fluttering madly. I counted the moths once. They were stationary for a whole minute. I reached thirty-seven and then they moved. They were watching me. Only a few were left to count. So now I count the tube lights in my house. I know there are eight and I can never go wrong. But I wish I had someone to live with so I could know for certain if they were growing in length.

I sit by the window and eat boiled potatoes. I am down to my last potato. My diet has changed since the loss of my arm. I eat poorly. By that I mean I eat food that is meant only for the poor. It does not seem right for a cripple to eat rich food. A suffering man cannot have a fat, happy face. I feel like a vegetable and so I must eat one.

The tenants in my building think I am poor. I am not. My parents were rich, but they got divorced. When they separated, they bought separate houses. When they died alone and separately, they left both the houses to me, which I sold. It is no success story, but it worked (and so I do not). They married late, had me late, and died early.

They had good manners. I thank them for sending me to private school. Other than that, I would like to keep things under the coffin.

There is a knock on the door. It scares me, but that is not unusual. I am always scared. Of telephone bills, the news, cycles, barbers, man-holes. The list goes on like a blind man circling the earth. I call it mandatory fear, or fear out of good manners. The tables have four legs; the chairs have four legs. The clock works, the telephone rings, the water quenches your thirst and the newspaper is tucked in your door latch each morning. You then prey upon your own house and lift the carpet to check for scorpions. You place your hand on your heart—has it left you? It is the way of humans, of a car that can move only backward. When the car finally hits a tree, the man is relieved even though the steering wheel is stuck in his chest.

I open the door. It is the garbageman. I shake my head to indicate I have nothing to deposit in his large cane basket which contains orange peels, eggshells and used tea leaves. The man hoists the basket on his shoulder and leaves. One day he will come to collect garbage and I will not be here. I will be under the earth. It is true that we are sinking. The thousand oil lamps have not made me feel lighter. I have been given a finger. It will lead me to my arm — lep-rous or torn off an ancient tree. It does not matter. It is a lead, and a lead is more than the stump I have.

On the other side of the street, barbers clip away at the heads of men. They snip in thin air most of the time. We all do. At night, even though the barbers are asleep, I can still hear the snipping. A man with a handcart carrying gas cylinders trudges past; the veins on the man's hands are green streams. He licks his own sweat, drinks his own dream. He will push for miles and stop to ask the time. Looking at the man makes me sink ten inches into the ground.

Once more there is a knock. It comes from the lower part of the door. Once more, I am scared. This time it is the fear you feel when you have been told that the earthquake will not hit your city. Why would God spare *you*? You have done nothing holy; you have not poured milk over his idol. God will send you a gift worse than an earthquake — a dead nightingale in your lap, a child carrying a hand grenade in your garden, an old lady calling you by the name of her dead son.

But I like opening doors. It is an activity that requires a single arm. You never use two hands to twist a doorknob or open a latch. I pick my tasks carefully.

Behind the door is a man sitting on his haunches, his hands clasped under his chin. A large cane basket lies on the ground before him. Its lid rattles with the flap of wings. He is selling chickens.

"What a great day to buy a chicken!" he shouts.

At least he gets straight to the point, unlike the milkman, who always asks me how my arm is. I just shake my head. But he continues to ask.

"My chickens are the size of dogs," says the man. His shoes are long and pointy, and curl upward at the tips.

"That's large," I say. "But no thank you." A door-to-door chicken salesman is unusual. Plus it is too early in the morning to talk. But after my two-month silence, the words want to burst out.

"For your wife," he says to me.

He deftly points to the lid of the basket as though its contents are top secret. Maybe he thinks the chickens do not know they are being sold.

"I don't have a wife," I tell him.

"Then what better way to get one?"

I want to say there are ten men in a room and all are women. Or that cemeteries would be wonderful if they did not have dead people. Two people not making sense are always better than one.

"Wives love chickens," says the man. "Buy a chicken and you will soon get a wife."

"No one will marry me," I say.

"Why not?"

"I'm a cripple."

"I would marry a cripple," he says. "If I loved her."

"I would not," I tell him truthfully.

"Then definitely buy a chicken."

"Why?"

"To eat," he says. "Why else?"

"I don't eat chicken. I'm vegetarian."

"If you tell me you are a trapeze artist I will believe you. But you are no vegetarian."

"What makes you say that?"

"I can tell by the way the chickens act. Notice how hard they flap? They want to escape. If you were a vegetarian they would be totally calm."

"I'm not hungry," I say.

"You're being ungrateful," he says. "There are children in hungry countries who would die for these."

"Then fly your chickens there," I say.

"Please buy one," he says. "I've not eaten since yesterday."

"Not eaten?"

"I've not made a sale."

"Why don't you eat your chickens?"

"I'm vegetarian," he says.

I want to close the door but I am afraid I will have to open it again.

"I have a solution," he says. "Use these chickens to do black magic. My chickens are specially suited for hexes."

"I do not wish to do black magic on anybody," I say.

I have heard of these spells, using lemons, chillies, chickens, hair and nails. It is a thriving business for some people. They place ads in newspapers. They are a bunch of moons thinking — after dark, before common sense.

"Better you do it on them before they do it on you. Take my advice, start collecting chickens."

"It's all rubbish!" I say.

"You are a man of little faith."

"It's a sin to do black magic."

"But everyone does it," he says. "Even them," he whispers.

"Your chickens?"

"They have cast the evil eye upon me many times. That's why they are in a basket. Otherwise what kind of salesman would not put his products on display?"

"The chickens are doing black magic. The cows are praying for us. This whole city is hanging upside down from monkey bars."

"You do not believe in BM?" he asks.

"BM?"

"Black magic."

"It's new to me," I reply.

He has changed the position in which he sits. The white lungi he wears is of thin cloth, shaping the bulb of his manhood.

"I will open the lid just a little. Look them right in the eye. It's like staring into an evil cave," he says.

I sit on my haunches exactly like the chicken-seller. The chickens flap so hard it seems as if they are trying to save themselves from drowning.

"Aren't they delicious?" he asks. "I'm a vegetarian and my mouth is watering."

"I thought you were going to show me their evil eye."

He sticks his forefinger out and licks it. His expression conveys that it is delightfully tasty. He is as joyous as the man who eats summer. He even bites lightly on his finger and makes the tip-top sign.

The moment he bites his own finger, I know it is a sign.

"The finger!" I shout. "You know about the finger!"

"Of course," he says. "Who doesn't?"

"Thank God," I say. "I had no idea what to do with it."

"So you will buy a chicken?"

"For the information you have, I will buy *all* of them."

"All?"

"All, my friend."

"You're not vegetarian?"

"It's a sin to be vegetarian."

"You want to buy all my chickens?" he repeats.

"Even the basket. But *only* if you give me my next clue."

"What clue?"

"Stop acting!"

"Baba, I'm not acting!"

"Baba! You said *Baba*."

"So what?"

"Are you Baba Rakhu?"

"Who?"

"You even bit your finger exactly like the leper did!"

"But it's very normal to lick your fingers to show how tasty your chicken is! It's not top secret!"

"Is that all you meant?"

He is silent.

I am silent.

I look outside the window. A boy on a cycle that is too big for him goes past. He leans forward and sits on the bar while riding it. An old newspaper is tucked under the carrier lid on the back of the cycle.

"I will leave the entire basket for you," the chicken-seller says. "It will cost you five hundred rupees."

Even lettuce leaves think more clearly than I do.

He pushes the basket through the door and leaves it at my feet. He thanks me as one would thank a mad person for giving directions. He has hustled chickens successfully, but does not know how he did it.

It is noon now and the chickens have tormented me all morning. As I rock back and forth on my wooden easy chair, they peep at me through the holes in the basket. Each time I nod off, they laugh loudly as if they have never seen a cripple nap before. Perhaps I should tear off one of their legs and see if they find it funny. I have been unable to leave their side. They need to be kept under constant surveillance. The chicken-seller was right. The chickens *are* doing black magic.

Black cockroaches emerge, one by one, from inside the basket. Brown cockroaches are good. Black ones are bad. Black ones sometimes pretend they cannot fly. So they crawl like tiny old men, begging and coughing, in the hope that you will feel sorry for them. As you bend down to support them, they fly straight into your eyes and rest in your cornea. They change the color of your eyes. From then on, everything appears dark. If you go to a circus, the clowns wear black smiles; if you attend a wedding, the bride wears a dark cloak; even freshly squeezed orange juice turns black right before your eyes. But they are not *your* eyes. The black cockroaches are seeing for you.

I shut my eyes tight so they have nothing to fly to. I think only of white things. The heart of a child, the cloth that covers a dead body before it is burnt, an old woman's steel hair, a star following its white reflection in a river. Before I open my eyes, I tell myself the black cockroaches are gone.

And they are.

I will wait for the brown ones I like.

I must put an end to the chickens or they will use their evil charms on the entire city. Soon millions of people will gather around chicken baskets and be laughed at by poultry. We have butchered them through the centuries, and now it is their turn to put us in tiny cells. They will feed us seeds, and watch us eat and shit. They will transport us in trucks and we will be scared to death. Then they will feast on us.

I lift the lid of the basket very slightly and take a peek. I do not know how many chickens are in there. Maybe five or six. I am outnumbered, but then battles are never even. I must find and slay their leader. The rest will lose heart and lie on the battlefield with their weapons by their sides.

It is a king's stare that separates him from his subjects. The chicken-seller spoke of an eye that was an evil cave. The one with that eye is their king.

As I peek in, the chickens all burst into flight. Feathers are lost, positions are exchanged and a wall is built. I peer into six pairs of eyes, still as beads on a rosary.

The first pair is too bright; these eyes have not been dimmed by life. They cannot be the king's eyes. The second pair is covered by curtains that have been lowered slowly with each passing year. These eyes choose to overlook the perils of a kingdom. The next are too greedy, full of rich sweets and false praise. They must be the food taster's. It is the fourth chicken that I must destroy. A king always has his food taster by his side.

I can see into the evil cave.

I place my hand into the basket and catch his neck. I can feel the fire in his throat rise like a flame fed by gasoline. I squeeze hard and the other chickens tear at my hand. I pull him closer to me and place a leg on the basket so that the others cannot escape.

I squeeze hard and bend his neck. In my palm I feel the last burst of life, a shot in the dark, a bullet traveling that extra inch. I break his neck; it snaps. I let go and pull my arm out. My hand is bloody and tired. The king is dead.

I pull the dead king out of his basket. He does not look the sorcerer now, just a dead bird. His eyes are still open. I must shut the entrance into the evil cave forever. As I glide my hands over the chicken's eyes to close the lids, I realize what I am doing. It is what the lady of the rainbow spoke of. I have found a way to close the evil eye that was cast upon me. There is not a sound from the basket. The storm has been lifted.

LIFE OF A DARK BLUE FILMMAKER

Now that the chickens have been destroyed, I am able to venture outside. It is strange what one night without sleep can do to you. Your hearing improves. I can hear my heartbeat. It skips. This means my heart is happy. But it does not mean *I* am happy. The pursuit of happiness is dangerous. Look at my heart. It is happy and so it skips. If by chance it falls down while skipping, it will hurt itself. It will be in pain. To its surprise, the pain will not die down. If the pain lasts for a prolonged period of time, the heart suffers an attack. So please understand that you can die from too much happiness.

I go back to Jalebee Road. The narrow lane that leads to the In-charge's beedi shop looks like any other. Vegetable vendors sell onions, tomatoes, cauliflower and lettuce from brown baskets. At least their products are on display, not banished under lids for being evil. The road is sticky. Dead vegetables are mashed into the ground. Rust-colored cycles rush past, the tring-tring of their bells reminding you of when you got your first ride, double seat on your servant's cycle. A scooter chokes on its owner again. The owner will try and kickstart it to no avail. Once a scooter chokes, it is dead for the day. Little children dressed in stolen clothes wait for instructions from beggar masters. There is soot in the air, but I see no chimneys. Only the factories have them. I have always wanted a chimney at home.

The In-charge cleans the counter with a white cloth. On seeing me, he turns his back and wipes the mirror that serves as a backdrop to his little cigarette shop. A flying chariot is embossed on the glass. In the mirror I see my empty sleeve. It hangs like a hollow pipe.

"What are you doing here?" he asks me.

"I have closed the evil eye. What must I do now?"

"With what?"

"The finger. I have brought it with me."

I show him the brown paper bag in my hand. He cleans the wheels of the chariot. The cloth makes a squeaking sound against the glass. A short man wearing tight white trousers and a ribbed red vest approaches. He places a black videocassette, without its cover, on the counter and taps his fingers on the wood.

"Gold Flake ka pack," he says. He looks in the mirror and combs his hair with his hands.

"Is it any good?" the In-charge asks him, using his chin to indicate the cassette.

"*Love in Bombay*," he replies. "I know the director."

"I would not own to knowing the director of such a third-grade picture," says the In-charge. "I need a decent movie. To watch at home with the in-laws."

"You know I don't keep family pictures."

"I'm saying it in the hope that you will."

"But I have to make a living."

I look at the flower shop next to me. Four buckets containing red and white roses are placed on the floor. The water is dark as though night has been squeezed into the buckets. The In-charge hands the man a pack of Gold Flake.

"Put it on my account," the man says. "What's the total?"

"More than you are worth."

"I think today you are after me. Did I say something to upset you?"

"It's enough that the movies you rent out are humiliating."

"What are you saying? *Love in Bombay* is a masterful picture. The Thok-Thak Brothers are pioneers in Indian vulgarity. It's a crime not to see their pictures."

"Third-class movie makers!"

"Boss, what you saying? Their movies are complete classics! Have you not seen *Life of a Dark Blue Filmmaker*? It will excite your blood to boiling point and beyond!"

"I saw *Bombay Buttocks*. The woman takes fifteen minutes to remove her pallu. She's so afraid to show her face."

"It begins slowly but then she is completely full-to. She just needed encouragement."

"Go rent your movies to your filthy customers," says the In-charge as he extends his hand to receive payment.

"So you want *Love in Bombay* for tonight or no?" The man smiles as he takes out a cigarette and taps it on the pack.

"I warn you, if it is as bad as *Bombay Buttocks,* I will stop selling you cigarettes."

"Don't worry. In this one, the woman is not wearing a pallu. She is full-to from the beginning."

"That's better," says the In-charge as he withdraws his hand.

"Take this tape with you and put another name on it so that my wife does not suspect. I will collect it in ten minutes from your house."

"What name to put?"

"*Documentary of Rare Birds.*"

The man performs a slight salaam to the In-charge, picks up the cassette and leaves.

"Who was that?" I ask.

"The local saint."

I deserve that answer. So I get to the point: "Are you going to help me or not?"

"With what?"

"I don't know what to do with the finger. You were the one who told me to take it since it was a mark of respect."

"You must leave now."

"I'm not going anywhere."

"Okay," he says. He leans toward me. I look into his eyes. They are large and brown, like a woman's. "Give me the finger."

I remove it from the brown paper bag. I am about to place the finger on the wooden counter.

"You will defile it if you place it there," he says sternly. He reaches below the counter. His cupped hand reveals an earthen bowl. "Put the finger in this bowl."

I place it in the bowl. He looks at it, deliberates. "There's something missing. Can you tell me what that is?" he asks.

"I don't know."

"Water."

"Water?"

"Yes. But I don't have any."

I point to the Bisleri bottle neatly tucked in a corner, right next to the hundred-page notebooks. This shop has everything. If I want to buy a midget, there will be one under the counter.

"It's unopened," he says. "I don't want to break the seal."

"I will buy it from you. But is the water really necessary?"

"It's crucial. It is very negligent of you not to have thought of this on your own."

I pay the In-charge ten rupees. He strips the blue seal off the bottle and pours water into the bottle cap until it overflows.

"The right amount must be administered," he tells me. He pours a few drops onto the finger.

"What are you doing?"

"Watering the finger."

"Why?"

"So it can grow into an arm."

I notice that he is not smiling. He leans close to me and whispers. "Plant this finger in your garden. Each time you water it, ask it to forgive you. When you have truly repented, it will grow into an arm."

"Is such a thing possible?"

"Of course not!" he roars with laughter. "What a sample!"

"You will never understand what it's like to lose an arm."

"Now go back," he says.

"Not until you give me my next clue."

"I just did."

"What do you mean?"

"Go back. Far back."

EMPTY WHISKEY BOTTLES

The finger could grow into an arm. I have to fight hard not to believe this. Loss of any kind is horrible. Not because it takes away, but because it makes you believe — in newspapers, in tomatoes, in empty whiskey bottles.

I am back at home now. The long walk from the In-charge's shop has tired me. The afternoon sun shines through my window as the barbers opposite my building smoke with the taxi drivers. They share cigarettes and stories. They are all short and thin. Each time they blow out smoke, they shrink in size. Each time they tell a story, they become thinner. When they sleep at night, they return to their normal size.

It is sad that people who have money do not live in these parts. They will never know the truth about barbers and taxi drivers. Until two months ago, I had never entered a barbershop. It is my mother's fault. She frequented *salons* and took me with her when I was little (it was her way of bonding with me). Although I despised spending time with her, I loved it when women with fluffy breasts would shampoo my hair, and massage my scalp with a stream of hot water. I had visions of biting into their flesh, of letting them pull out my hair, strand by strand, instead of cutting it. Such was my desire for those fluffy-breasted hair cutters. After the haircut, they would smile and ask if I wanted anything else. When I told them what I wanted, they would chide me with a slap on the wrist. You naughty boy, they would say. You'll grow up and be a terror.

But the barbers opposite my building cut off only those strands that have split out of guilt, or gone white out of fear. These strands fall to the ground until they are swept away by a cheap broom. That is why you always feel better after a haircut. But only if you have the right barber. When your hair grows back, so does the guilt and fear. I now have haircuts every week.

I am too tired to take a nap. So I have lined forty empty whiskey bottles in a row on the floor. When I lost my arm, I stopped drinking. But I carried these whiskey bottles from my old flat to the new one. Even though they contain nothing, I cannot throw them away. They were drunk in the past, over nights, days, funerals, weddings, and card sessions. They are not empty — they hold my past.

Yet, it is not what these bottles hold, but what once held them that stops me from smashing them all. My left arm, the one I lost. You eat with the right; you sign and shake hands with the right, but you always drink and smoke with the left. The right is your life; the left is your death. Never mix the two. As long as your right does not know what the left does, you will continue living.

The answer to my quest lies in my past. I must go back, far back, as the In-charge said. I will invoke my past by stroking an empty whiskey bottle. For the first time in my life, I hold a whiskey bottle with my right hand. Maybe it does not matter. For even if you have drunk only water, your manner can still suggest you have consumed bottles and bottles of whiskey.

I am always the first one to run through the corridor when the bell rings. I rush to the water tank to drink the contaminated water. It is not boiled. It is not filtered. There is surefire bravery in drinking it. Even though I get to the row of taps before my classmates do, I wait for them to show up. They must see me drink this water. I pull my red school tie over my shoulder so that it does not get wet when I bend down to cup the water in my hand. But even the seniors are not drinking water today. Maybe no one is thirsty.

The first few sips always taste like fresh lake water, but today seems different. I quench my thirst, make sure that the dryness in my throat is gone. I look outside and see that the walls of the church are being painted. They stopped taking our class to church after we were caught changing the words of all the hymns.

There is a tap on my back. "Did you not hear what Miss said to the class?"

It is Viren, worthless Viren.

"No cloud, no rain, it's only Viren," I shout. Viren, who wears a yellow tie, has yellow teeth, whose gumboots are also yellow. Just like a girl's gumboots.

I wipe the water off my lips but let the tie stay over my shoulder, unlike Viren's. His tie is as well behaved as a picnic photo.

"Did you not hear what Miss said?" he asks again.

"Which Miss?" I ask.

"Miss Bardet."

"Did she tell the class about your mother?"

Viren's tie stiffens. No cloud, no rain, and still Viren is upset. "Go to hell," he says. "I will not tell you what she said."

Viren turns and leaves. I do not like this. I must use some fancy English to irritate Viren. It is his favorite subject.

"I *forbid* you to leave," I say.

Viren turns and looks my way. There are no bruises on his face. The bastard is beginning to heal fast. He likes to read and write. He keeps a diary.

"Come here," I say.

"Otherwise?"

"Otherwise I will tell Shakespeare."

I find that funny. Viren does not. I do not know Shakespeare, but Viren talks about him all the time. I do know that he is fancy and English. Apart from that, I am guessing he must be a family relative with lots of money. No, wait; I remember Viren quoting one of Shakespeare's sayings. The fool must be a writer.

The only thing I like about Viren is that he is stubborn. Even though he is a girl, he is a stubborn one. He never learns that it is bad to answer back.

"Now tell me what Miss Bardet said," I demand.

"Nothing."

His face begins to crumple as if he is anticipating a slap. I begin to feel sick. There must have been something in the water. I want to vomit but not in front of Viren. Maybe *on* Viren, but not in front of him.

Now a few students have stepped out and are talking in the corridor. I see Rahul and his sister, also the fat girl from the other division with her pink lunch box. Viren turns around and sees them. There is also that new boy, who wears short pants, standing in the doorway. I will deal with him later.

I catch Viren by the collar and make sure that everyone is watching.

"Let me go," says Viren.

"Okay," I say. I let go of his collar and yank his tie so hard, the knot becomes the size of a tiny ball.

"Now, Viren, tell me what Miss Bardet said."

"No."

I pull harder. No cloud, no rain, but every vein in his neck is choking up. I do not want him dead, so I loosen the grip.

"She said in class that a dead rat is in the water tank and that no one must drink the water."

I let go of his tie. I feel even more sick. Miss Bardet takes the first class each morning. How can she expect us to pay attention at such an early hour?

Viren turns around and loudly announces, "He drank the dead-rat water. He drank the dead-rat water."

Rahul and his sister laugh, the new boy in short pants laughs, the fat girl laughs, and I am sure her pink lunch box finds it funny, too. Viren runs back toward the class. I must catch him before he tells the whole world.

I run after him and slap him hard on the back and he falls to the concrete floor. His pretty yellow gumboots squeak as I drag him back to the water tank. I think of the dead rat lying on its back, floating in the water tank. If I throw up before beating him, I will never be able to study in this school again. Then all the new boys will wear short pants and no one will be there to stop them.

I put Viren's head under the water taps and open two of them. Viren tries hard to get up but I push his chest against the parapet so that he cannot breathe. I turn his head so that his mouth is directly under the water flow, and I can see the tears. Soon they will be washed off with dead-rat water.

"Open your mouth," I tell him.

"Please . . ." His voice shakes.

"Drink the water. Fast."

I force open his mouth and watch the water gush in. Viren is crying and his hair is wet. He will get punished in class for this. Too much rain for Viren. As I squeeze his neck hard, I wonder how anyone can wear yellow gumboots.

As I caress the bottle, I look outside. Smells travel through the air. Of fried onions, from the plate of a cook to a hungry house. Of failure, as a man sends a letter to his wife in the village, explaining how he lost his job. Of parting, as a dead son rises through the dust and waves goodbye to his mother.

I raise the bottle to my nose and inhale the dank smell of whiskey. There is dust on the bottle mouth, which I wipe with my hand. I cut myself on the glass. The mouth is sharp and angry. It feels good. Blood trickles down the bottle. A few drops fall in. Where there once lived whiskey, there is blood. But the two know each other well — there is a lot of whiskey in my bloodstream.

As I watch the drops fall, I understand what my next step should be.

My past has drawn blood. It is what I must do to my present. I must suck my own blood until there is none left.

I must kill myself.

THE RULE OF WIDOWS AND MAD DOGS

There is an unwritten rule, or, if it is writ, it lies sculpted on God's arm. Once your journey begins, you cannot end it. You can propel yourself off track, skid in different mud, but it will only make your journey that much longer. There is another rule, that of widows and mad dogs. It lies under their beds. God has never read it for he does not visit their homes. I will find out which rule holds true.

I do not have the proper tools for the test, but my qualifications are excellent. The rich succeed at suicide but not because they are adept at it. They have the facilities: the guns and expensive rope. They live in tall buildings from which they can jump. But if I jump from the ground floor, it will be like trying to drown a fish.

I am not skillful with knives. I might cut the wrong vein, slash my throat at an inappropriate angle and bleed insufficiently. In my delirium, I will be too weak to cut again. I might be rescued by a misguided individual who means well. That would be tragic.

I walk to the kitchen, to where the rectangular grinding stone rests on the floor. I wear white, the color of death. Before death, our faces go white. The hospitals we die in have white walls, white sheets, nurses and doctors who wear white. The bedpans and bowls we spit our sickness into are white. Even the stray dogs that walk the hospital grounds are white. I am dressed for the occasion.

I wish the grinding stone was not black. I lift it a little and rest it on my thigh. It is very heavy. I tuck it under my arm and walk to the door. Even though I have money for a taxi, I want to take a bus. It will make my death seem more tragic. If God is not paying attention, he will think I am poor — a public transit user. I will get extra points in heaven. God favors those who travel by bus and train. The reason is simple — he sympathizes with them. In fact, hell's design is loosely based on a railway platform: no urinal, lots of people, and you have to buy a ticket even though you do not want to be there.

What is wrong with me? I am about to die. I must speak kindly of God.

Thinking about God has suddenly drawn my attention to my fatty bank account. I will certainly not donate any money to the poor. If I give them money, I am tampering with karma. I do not wish to alter God's work.

Let them remain poor. He wants it so.

Let the bank managers worry about what to do with my mutual funds, provident funds, drinking funds, and my weekly prostitute allowance. They will wait for relatives to come and make a claim, but no one will step forward because I am known as a drinker and as a bad man who goes to bad women, and they want nothing to do with me. As the months pass, my relatives will tell themselves that all that money lying in the bank is a terrible waste. So they will fight over it and there will be more death.

I wish I could leave a legacy. It is most important. Even though you die, your work must live on. But I have never worked in my life.

It is a dreadful thought, really. Work. The only thing that sounds more depressing is marriage.

But doing nothing also takes a lot of work. Trust me, I know. It was very hard for me to wake up seven days a week and do nothing. So I slept two days at a time. I was a master at it. I do have my reasons for not working. I was either in a brothel, or I was thinking about being in a brothel; I was either drunk, or I was thinking about getting drunk. When I look back, my time was well spent.

Who would have thought that a bright child like me would turn out this way? It makes my heart bleed. "He comes from a privileged background," they used to say. His father's a surgeon. (But the poor man used to cut himself while shaving. That they did not know.) His mother's a lawyer. (She had an affair with a Supreme Court judge for years. That they *did* know. I found out when I came home from school one day.)

They gave me lots of money. They were good parents. But love is overrated. I would take hundred-rupee notes over hugs and kisses any day.

As I wait for the bus outside the iron gates of my building, flying cockroaches come toward me. They are graceful in flight, like dancers. They are good and brown. The afternoon sun coats them with light. They fly in peace during the day, and at night a few of them, older ones, circle the stars and name them.

An old man joins me at the bus stop. He stares at the grinding stone I carry. This man has one arm, he must think; why does he carry a grinding stone? I will pose my own question: If we have two eyes, why do we close one when aiming a gun? Or wink? Why not wink with both eyes? Why use only one leg to kick and one hand to slap? That is why we have been given just one heart.

If we had a pair, one would remain unused and closed.

I wonder if the old man sees the flying cockroaches.

From around the corner emerges the dark shadow of a red double-decker bus. The bus tilts to one side, a curse waiting to fall on the street. I have been told this tilt is necessary and scientifically sound, that my worry is ridiculous. The bus charges toward us even though the driver knows he has to stop.

I let the old man get on first. He takes very small steps. I must act quickly or else the bus will leave without me. There is a boarding area, a square that is always crowded by standees. One must get onto it in seconds or wait for the next bus only to meet with the same fate. Old people, children, and cripples are damned. The god of public transit does not indulge in frivolity. For sentiment and mush, please visit your local cinema hall.

I squat a little, squeeze the grinding stone under my arm even tighter and leap onto the bus. I land. This grinding stone is too heavy. Why did I keep it? I do not have a servant to use it for grinding masalas. But it is useful in death.

I look for a seat. It is midafternoon so the workers are still in the factories, the housewives are done with the daily bazaar, and only the jobless ride the bus, the bags under their eyes filled with the sorrow of the world.

I sit with the grinding stone in my lap. The bus conductor approaches. He rubs his way through the passengers, his body scraping the fronts, sides and especially the backs of women (and sometimes men). He wears a brown uniform that chars him in the city heat. The government has given him a brown leather pouch to collect change from the passengers. Brown skin, brown uniform, brown pouch. Who says we are not organized? Such cohesion cannot be the outcome of the Third World.

I have a suggestion. To avoid confusion, countries should be numbered on the map: First World, Second World, Third World. This way, travel agents cannot fool poor foreigners. Madam, I promise you we are a First World country. So what if there are flies and malaria? A little sickness is good for health. Who said we don't have water? Forget water, we have water buffaloes. No electricity? What you are talking, madam! If we did not have electricity, would I be shocked at your questions?

Okay, madam, I will not lie. At least we came in Third.

The bus conductor looks at the grinding stone as I remove change from my pocket to buy a ticket. This man has one grinding stone, he must think. Why does he carry an arm? Bus conductors are known to think differently.

I hand him the coins.

"Which stop?" he asks.

"Last stop," I reply.

"Next time, exact change," he says.

"No next time," I say. "Today I am suicide!"

But he has already moved on to the next victim. The bus rumbles along, hits potholes and taps the occasional cyclist. Through the window I see the city pass by like an old postcard. The streetlights bend toward us and potholes grow larger; they spread like blotches of ink. Bridges hinge on the brink of collapse. They will fall when the maximum number of pedestrians and vehicles cross over them. I could sit on a bridge all day and wait for it to fall. But that would take time. The magazine vendors come up to the taxis, showing off dark-skinned beauties on the covers, only a few rupees for an afternoon of hand pleasure. Maya, Mamta, Sushma and Padma. Beautiful names that have lent their bodies for the public good.

I hear drumbeats. The bones of my severed hand are being used as drumsticks. The sound is everywhere, but only those who have lost a limb can hear it. I see an ivory drum in the center of the street, right next to the cobbler's stand. People walk by as if they do not see the ivory drum. One-armed, one-legged men beat the ivory with the femurs of cripples. This is the sound where life and death meet. Have a small chat, a cup of tea, and decide who shall recede or encroach for the moment. I hope death is persuasive. Suicide, you are all I have left.

The last stop is just before the old burnt-down mill.

I get off the bus and face the sea.

I turn around and face a tall building. It is under construction. I shall plunge to my death from the twentieth floor. The grinding stone is crucial to my plans. I am not very heavy. Okay, I am light. From time to time, muscles do sprout from my arms, chest and legs, but they are fleeting. They always succumb to sickness and injury.

The grinding stone will make me travel with greater velocity. The time it takes to travel twenty storeys can be especially long if, during the fall, one has second thoughts about dying. The greater the velocity, the harder the impact. The harder the impact, the more efficient the spread of skull on pavement. I shall make the clean-up job difficult for officials.

The racetrack of my life will be laid out for them. They will know I have gone off course, over the rails. To my left, they will find the arm that I leave behind. After I am dead, it might live on and do some good.

I enter the building and take the lift. There is no one around, so I go unnoticed. My arm aches from the weight of the stone. I get off on the terrace. The day is still gloomy. I climb onto the ledge and face the sea. The wind hits the sleeve of my lost arm and it flutters like a white sail. I watch it move gracefully as though it never needed an arm to fill it. The sleeve is my solitary wing. I will fly to my death. But I will have to make an extra effort to avoid the scaffolding.

I look straight ahead. Somewhere, in the country on the other side of this great sea, someone else commits suicide. He looks at the same sea, thinks the same thing. I am with you, my friend. I hope you have a grinding stone, too. I have left the city, moved out of the forest into the clearing. I can never go back. I know I will jump.

"Hero, what are you doing?"

It is a worker on the scaffolding. I stare at his skinny legs. He squats on the scaffold like it is on the ground floor.

"Were you about to jump?" he asks.

He has the eyebrows of an eagle. I feel compelled to answer.

"Yes," I say.

"What is that stone for?"

"The stone is for speed."

"Okay, best of luck."

"What?"

"Hurry up. I don't have all day."

"You will not stop me?"

"What for? Your decision."

Wisdom is a squatting eagle on a scaffold, an eagle who works for less than minimum wage. The signs are clear. I will succeed. The rule of widows and mad dogs shall prevail. So it *is* possible to end one's journey.

"One question," he says.

"Speak, my friend." I feel jubilant.

"Where is the note?"

"What note?"

"Suicide note!"

I do not appreciate being reminded that I have overlooked a telling detail before death.

"You forgot note? You don't watch TV at home?"

"I . . ."

"Not to worry. Do it now."

"On what?"

"Oral. Recite to me. I am your audience."

"No, I . . ."

"Please start."

His eyebrows arch and I am compelled once more.

I blabber: "Dear Friends . . ."

"You have friends?" he asks.

I do not. This is disastrous. "Dear World . . ."

"If the world is dear to you, why are you leaving it?"

"What shall I say?"

"Be insulting. Give bad words."

"Sewer of a city," I say.

"Excellent. Well put. You are on your way."

"May the palms of your hands be stained with the blood of a thousand lepers."

"You are a poet. Tagore, boss."

"May the teeth of your wisdom fall in the winter of your stupidity."

"I wish I had a pen. You are gifted. It is sad that you will be dead."

"I am a gem in your stone. May you choke on the smoke of your own sadness."

The man applauds. "True class," he says.

I bow. Twenty storeys high, and it is effortless. They say grace comes before death. I believe it. If only wisdom came to the living. When death comes, we all walk like lions and wish the earth well.

"Before you go," the worker says, "I would like to touch that stone. A mark of respect to you."

I am flattered. The respect of a worker is hard to earn. I very cautiously hand him the grinding stone.

"It is heavy. Oh, it is heavy . . ."

He is off balance. I reach out to hold him; I extend my left arm. The problem is, I do not have one.

"Don't leave the grinding stone!" I shout.

The man falls and bursts like a watermelon. He has stolen the vehicle of my death.

The wind carries his last words to me. "To those who find me," he says, "I have this to say. We worship the wrong people, we shake the wrong hands, and we eat the bread that is not laid out for us."

Suicide, you do not exist.

MADAM AND BOMBER

Death walks in front of me; it knows I am chasing it, so it does its best to evade me. Life knows I fear it, so it runs behind me and hides in shadows and corner shops, out of sight but close enough for me to smell. There is a place on earth where life and death meet. It is called a Job. I must find that place.

Back at home, I stare at my telephone.

It is an old-fashioned telephone, black and boxy. I hold the receiver between neck and shoulder and dial the number listed under "Government Inquiries." Since I am miserable anyway, I wish to work for the government. After nine rings, a lady answers the phone.

"Madam, I want to find out about government jobs," I say.

"What type of job?" she asks.

"Any job. But it has to be for the government."

"What number you want?"

I quote the number in the phone book.

"This number is out of order," she says.

"How can it be out of order if I am talking to you?"

"Are you being smart?"

"I just want to find out about a government position."

"Then call the right number," she insists. "You want anything else?"

"Madam, the right number."

"You have pen-pencil?"

Without waiting for me to respond, she fires the number at me. So I call the new number, the one that is not out of order. Again a lady picks up.

"Madam, I want to find out about government jobs," I ask.

"Didn't you just call?"

It is the same lady. "Madam, you gave me this number."

"Am I saying no, or what? What is the problem?"

"There is no problem. I just want to work for the government."

"Why? You have criminal record?"

"Madam, please, I am not a criminal."

"Then what? Tell the truth."

"I'm a cripple."

"That is not good. Now, what job you are looking for?"

"Anything that is open."

"This is a restaurant or what? Be direct. Government time not to be wasted."

"I wish to be a suicide bomber," I state.

"A who?"

"One who blows his own bomb," I reply.

"Is this a terrorist call?"

"No, I . . ."

"If this is a terrorist call, there is separate number for that."

"I'm not a terrorist."

"Then what you are saying? Listen, you are eating my lunch break."

I look at the time. It is 3 p.m.

"Madam, I want to apply for the position of governmental suicide bomber."

"Are you insulting us? There is penalty for such acts. I warn you."

"I want to serve, not offend. Now listen: If you want someone dead and that person is not dying, I will do what you need by putting a bomb inside my shirt and then hugging that person."

"Why would I want anyone dead?"

"Not you, madam. *Them!*"

"Them who?"

"If I say, you will be offended."

"Forget it! You are nonsense. You ate half my lunch break! Call in fifteen minutes. Okay, what?"

"Just tell me when I can come for an interview. Should I bring a mock bomb?"

"What interview? We don't need a bomber!"

"Madam, of course you need one. Look at that Veerappan. For many many years he has been hiding in the forest smuggling sandalwood. He even kidnaps movie stars once in a while to earn extra pocket money. Now you cannot catch him. So let him kidnap me and then I will explode."

"Why will Veerappan kidnap you?"

"I will pretend to be an actor."

"How can cripple be actor?"

"I admire your memory."

"Are you giving me line? I am married-wedded."

"I am not giving you line. I am giving you a compliment. Now, what do you think of my idea?"

"Of hugging Veerappan?"

"Yes. Headline will say: 'Sandalwood Bandit Killed by Suicide Bomber.'"

"You will take all the focus. What about me?"

"We can say it was your idea, that you masterminded the whole thing. You will get a promotion and a house in Pune."

"You do not mind dying?"

"I mind more that I have to hug Veerappan. I cannot bear the smell of sandalwood. Look, I'm a cripple anyway. I want to go fast. But I want to serve the nation before I exit."

"I am beginning to understand what you are saying. Now, since you ate my full lunch break, call little later. I need to think about this. Do not speak with anyone else. We need code names. These phones are taped."

"Madam, yours is a government phone. Why is it tapped?"

"Not tapped. Taped. It is an old phone. There is brown tape on the dial."

"I am sorry."

"Okay, your code name is Suicide Bomber."

"Applicant," I add. "Because I have not got the job yet."

"Suicide Bomber Applicant." She lets the code name hang in the air. "No," she says. "It is too long."

"Okay," I reply. "And what is your code name?"

"You are cripple-donkey or what?"

"Madam?"

"Use name you have been calling me so far."

A little later:

"Suicide Bomber here."

"Madam speaking. Sorry. Plan flop."

"What?"

"My supervisor not agreeable."

"Madam, you are crushing my childhood dream."

"What do you mean? Since childhood you want to be suicide bomber?"

"No, since childhood I've wanted to die."

"If you were my son I would slap you!"

For a moment I visualize Madam seated on a desk surrounded by old files and papers, the black phone receiver tasting the oil of her black hair. I imagine thick glasses on a nose with flaring nostrils, portions of her belly folded and dead on her lap.

She carries on, "Government time not to be wasted."

"Forget bomber. Can you give me the number for psychological assistance?"

"Cycle what?"

"Mental-help number."

"What do you mean?"

"If I am distressed then who do I talk to?"

"No such number."

"There is no such care for the citizens of this country?"

"If there is such a number then everyone will call and phone lines will be jam."

"But I need help. I want to talk to someone."

"Call Mr. P. He will listen."

"Mr. P?"

"World-famous coffin maker. He is family friend."

"Are you joking?"

"Government does not joke. Tell him I told to call."

She gives me the number. I hang up.

✻

Immediately:

"Hello, Mr. P speaking."

"Can I speak with Mr. P?"

"Did I not say I'm Mr. P?"

"Sorry, you see . . ."

"Now, tell me who died."

"Nobody died."

"So you want the coffin for recreation?"

I must play along. Mr. P will not speak to me if I am not interested in coffins. "Yes," I say. "I want a coffin to sleep in. I have a strong family history of people dying in their sleep. So I do not want to inconvenience anyone with coffin measurements when it is my turn. I like to be organized."

"How tall are you?"

"Five seven or eight."

"Make up your mind."

"What difference will one inch make?"

"Ask your wife," Mr. P chuckles.

"Five seven," I say.

"Are you sure you are five seven? I do not want you to be uncomfortable."

"It will hardly matter when I am dead."

"But you will be sleeping in the coffin."

"Oh, correct. Yes, better make it five eight then."

There is the sound of traffic in the background and the sound of birds.

"Now. Color of your hair?" he asks me.

"Black. Why?"

"I want the inside of the coffin to match. Smoking or non-smoking?"

"Non."

"Do you want a lid now or at the time of death?"

"Now. I need complete darkness to sleep."

"We are ready, then. I need advance cash. Your name, please?"

"Suicide Bomber."

"What?"

"That is my name. Madam gave it to me."

"Madam who?"

"Your family friend."

"Listen, fellow, I do not know any Madam. Is this a joke?"

"Mr. P, I would never waste the time of a world-famous coffin maker like you."

"Good. Now about this bomber person . . ."

"That is my name. You see, it has been my dream since childhood."

"To be a bomber?"

"To die."

"You need help, Mister."

"Madam was right. You are the contact person."

"I don't know this Madam!"

"But you will help me."

"With what?"

"Madam said that you will give me Mental Health Support. Since there is no service provided for us citizens."

"Mental Health Support. What's that?"

"You need not pretend, Mr. P. Where shall I begin?"

"Nothing to begin! Now, do you want the coffin or not?"

"If you listen to me, I will buy the coffin."

"Please start. From the beginning."

"You see, Mr. P, I do not have an arm. So I tried to kill myself. But then this poor construction worker died instead of me when he grabbed my grinding stone to pay me respect."

"Did he have a coffin?"

"Who?"

"The worker. Did he have a proper coffin?"

"I don't think he did."

"An outrage," he says.

"My story, Mr. P."

"I apologize. Please carry on."

"So the worker fell from the twentieth floor and splattered. Then I could not kill myself, so I called Madam and she rejected my idea of hugging Veerappan."

"Why do you want to hug Veerappan?"

"So we both explode. Mr. P, you are not paying attention. As of now, I do not have a single foot in your coffin."

"Sorry. Please go into more detail."

"Okay. This leper gave me his finger. But I have no idea what it signifies."

"Everybody knows it is rude. There is no deeper meaning."

"No, Mr. P. Again you are not listening. He *physically* gave me the finger. Bit it off."

"Did it have a coffin?"

"The finger?"

"Yes. The finger coffin is like a cigarette case."

"Mr. P!"

"Damn you and your finger! I am the world's best coffin maker! I do not need this torture to make a sale!"

He puts the phone down. I put the phone down. The world is a cruel place. There is no room for cripples even though we occupy less space than full-formed humans do. I need Mental Health Support. There has to be someone who offers this service. I want Veerappan. I will hug him like he is my brother. Then I will calmly undo my shirt and explode.

AK MUNNA TIGER LILY

I storm out of my house with a brown paper packet clutched in my hand. I look to the sky in absolute delight, for I know that God is about to throw me an arm. Instead of rain, arms will fall to earth, separately and in pairs, in different colored skins, in various shapes and sizes. All cripples can pick and choose, and take a few home with them in case of damage or wear and tear. It is not my fault I think like this. There is a lack of Mental Health Support in this country.

There is too much traffic today. I see the barbers through their glass window, examining heads and beards, waiting for the taxi drivers to collect outside so they can have their next smoke. I weave through the crawling taxis, buses, handcarts and cycles until the sidecar of a scooter taps my leg. It is a wonder people still use these; they were famous during World War II. Entire families travel in them, and it would be no surprise to me if they also carried the family tree. Husband riding, wife behind him with a little baby in her arms, three older children in the sidecar, their heads bobbing up and down like circus clowns. It is a travesty the way parents transport their children.

I reach the concrete divider in the middle of the road. My brown paper packet has greasy samosa stains on it. A beggar child sits next to me and waits for the light to turn red. Three black and yellow taxis are stuck behind a water tanker, which has *Beware of Dreams* written on it. Why only dreams? It is better to be wary of everything.

Part of the road has been dug up, and a stray dog lies inside the pit along with his collection of metal tins, pieces of wood and a shop hoarding for Tip Top tailors. The only way the pit will be covered is if ten cyclists fall into it on their way to work.

I look at the little boy slouched next to my feet. His hands are circled around his knees as if he were his own mother, trying to provide love and comfort. A man tries to push his handcart through the space between the taxi and water tanker. A BEST bus now takes its place behind the third taxi.

As the light turns red, the boy runs to the nearest taxi. With a steady stream of discharge from his nose, he tries to lean his chin on the rear window. He is too short. In the backseat of the taxi is a large woman.

"In God's name," I hear the boy say. "Please give money."

I have heard these words in the past and they meant nothing to me. It made me angry that small children begged. If I do not feed them, I thought, they will die and I will be doing them a favor. If we all stopped giving alms, dead beggars would fall on the streets like flies. It will help our government. If outside countries want to help, they should send planes so we can load bags and bags of poor children on board. Then we will all feel better.

At this moment, even though the boy's words are the same as they have always been, even though I take them in through the same ears, I do not want him dead. I am listening through the arm I do not have. So it does not surprise me when the woman in the taxi ignores the small boy's words and shifts to the center of her seat.

She has two arms and that impairs her hearing.

"Only five rupees. Will eat food," he begs again.

"Five? You want to eat in a five-star?" she barks.

The boy's clothes are brown as the bag I hold and equally greasy. He puts his hand inside the taxi.

"I've not eaten for three days," he tells the woman.

The woman digs into her handbag. The boy rises on his toes and peers into the taxi. The woman pulls out a handkerchief from her handbag and dabs her forehead with it. Two short pats on the cheek later, she puts the handkerchief back into her bag. The boy's feet are flat on the burning concrete again.

"Give anything," he says.

I step off the divider and tap the boy's shoulder. Some time ago, it would have been to admonish or to dismiss. Two arms can be more selfish than one. I have used them in the past to prevent others from growing taller.

"Raju," I say.

I once heard that all beggar children like to be called Raju. They respond as if it is their name.

"Raju, that well is dry." I place the paper bag on the road. He smiles at me and nods his head. I dig into my pocket.

"You also don't take out handkerchief," he says.

I slap a five-rupee note into his palm. "Go eat in a five-star."

"For that I need five hundred," he replies.

I raise my hand as though I am about to hit Raju and he ducks. Before moving to the next taxi, Raju smiles my way. I have never had a Raju smile at me before. I have not given him reason to. I feel sad, as if I have found a remedy for a disease that has already killed me.

Suddenly horns are blaring ahead of me. A policeman is directing traffic and it is obvious from the position of the vehicles that the jam will take some time to clear. The handcarts and cycles have moved forward despite this. I pick the bag up from my feet and leer into the taxi.

When in doubt, suspend all logic. Slit common sense by the throat. Travel to the nearest newsstand and ask for elephants. Walk to the bakery and show complete disbelief when they inform you they do not stock piranha. It is the only way to find a use for that which has none: a leper's finger.

"Lady, can I interest you in some shopping?" I ask.

She does not respond. Instead she looks straight ahead.

"He does have a nice head, doesn't he?"

She looks my way, confused.

"The taxiwala. The back of his head looks quite . . . majestic," I state.

The taxiwala does not care that he is the subject of conversation. Maybe he is thinking of his village and the wife he left behind. There is a blob of phlegm on his windshield. Must have been a disgruntled passenger. Or the taxiwala's jilted lover.

I continue, "Lady, if I may point out, there are three to four droplets of sweat on his neck. While I agree *that* is not majestic, it's the shape of his skull that is most noteworthy."

"What do you want?" she finally spurts.

"I want to interest you in some shopping."

"No, thank you. Now leave before I call that policeman."

"But that is a traffic policeman. He can barely control cars. Human beings are out of the question."

"Driver, take the taxi in front," she demands.

The taxiwala turns and faces her. He looks at me but then decides that the sun is in his eyes and faces the wheel again.

"Did you not listen? This man is harassing me. Take the car in front."

"It's against the law to hit the car in front," he says. "Now, please remain calm until the traffic clears. As it is, I'm being boiled."

I step in again. "Lady, I have a great bargain for you. At least see what I'm selling."

"Whatever it is, I don't need it."

"I'm glad you are interested." I raise the brown paper bag to her eye level. The paper crinkles as I open it. "Lady, it's a finger."

She seems agitated and looks ahead to see if any cars are moving. I open the bag a little more and face it toward her. "How much are you willing to pay for this?"

She looks inside the bag. Her scream terrifies the taxiwala.

"What happened? Cockroach?" he inquires.

"This man has a black finger in his bag!"

"Black finger?" The taxiwala turns my way.

I close the bag. I might get beaten. A lady-scream can attract a mob, especially if a man inspires the lady-scream. But if the man is handicapped, the mob is confused. The mob is then divided between the lady and the cripple.

The flying cockroaches rescue me. They come in hordes, dark soldiers with blades spread; they whiz past my head. The taxiwala acts as if he does not see them. He wants me to think they are not real, that only I have dark friends who fly in hundreds.

"What black finger?" he asks the lady.

"A black finger is a word ladies use for cockroach," I interject.

"Ah." He seems satisfied.

"There's no cockroach! It's a real finger," the lady insists.

"That stupid handcart fellow!" bellows the taxiwala. "Who told him to go in between? Now at least ten more minutes' wait." He cranes his neck outside the window to get a better view.

I remove the finger from the bag and present it to the lady as though I am giving her a red rose. "Lady, how much will you give for this magnificent structure?" I ask.

She fiddles with her handbag again, this time struggling to reach in. She throws fifty rupees onto the driver's seat and flees the taxi from the other side.

"Is this taxi empty?" I ask the driver.

"Where you want to go?"

"I need to decide. I must look for my next clue," I tell him.

I listen for clues in the blaring of horns. But there is no pattern in the way they erupt; I can take hints only from things that are systematic. Maybe nature can direct me. There are small trees, very thin, planted on the sidewalk at regular intervals. The trees are bereft of leaves. That also means nothing. I look at the hot sky. It is so hot that one by one birds will burn and fall to the ground. On a charred wing, I will find words in my name. I will tear the wing off, secretly put it in my pocket and read it in the shade. But there is not a bird in the sky.

"What are you looking up for?" asks the taxiwala.

"An answer."

"The day the heavens give an answer, I will stop driving like hell."

"I don't think I will take your taxi. I have to wait here."

"For a plane?"

"For directions."

"Look ahead. The cars are moving. Get in fast."

"But I don't know where to go."

"All line clear," he says. "Just like Clear Road."

"Clear Road?"

"You don't know Clear Road?"

"No."

"It's near St. Bosco School at Byculla."

As soon as he mentions St. Bosco School, I open the door of the taxi and get in as if my life depends on its torn seat. "You mean *Clare* Road," I tell him. My heart is pounding so hard that women plucking tea leaves in Assam can hear it.

"*Clear* Road! It's given that name because it is one of the few roads in this city that has no traffic. All line Clear."

"Okay. Take me to Clear Road, then," I say.

My driver slides left on the seat, circles his arm through the open window and turns the meter to bring the fare back to minimum.

I look up at the sky and tell it that I do not need its birds to tell me where I must go next. "Stop outside St. Bosco School," I tell the driver.

"Careful. A lot of gangs are there."

"I know. I went to school with them."

"Were you beaten?"

"Lots," I lie.

"Then why go back to your school?"

"To show people my finger."

It makes perfect sense. Only a taxi driver can show me the way, tell me what road I must take. I am going back to my roots. I must go back to school, where I will learn something.

Viren is breathing heavily. The lid of his brown desk is open as he puts all his schoolbooks into his sweet little blue bag. Each of his notebooks is neatly marked: History, Geography, Mathematics,

Science, Moral Science. I do not see his English book. Perhaps he has given it to Shakespeare to read.

The rest of us are getting ready for the first period after the lunch break. The class is Moral Science. Marks from this class are not counted as part of the final grade, but the lectures have been added mainly for our class, since we were asked to leave the church and its beautiful hymns more than a year ago.

Viren sees me as he puts the last of his books into his bag. He does not take his eyes off me, but continues to wheeze hard. I approach him and start wheezing exactly like him. Now I have the class's attention. I must hurry before the teacher walks in with messages from Almighty God.

"You should become a yoga master," I tell Viren. "You breathe so well."

The girls in the class laugh and the boys gather closer to Viren's desk. Viren tries to gather courage.

"Can I be your disciple?" I ask. "Please, yogiji, I want to be your humble pupil."

Viren tries to put one hand through the strap of his blue bag. I snatch the bag away from him. He must be very tired, for he does not even resist. This is no fun.

"You accept me as your yoga student or not?" I ask.

He does not answer. The girls have stopped laughing. The boys are bored.

"Okay," I say. "I will prove to you that I am worthy, that I can breathe as superbly as you do."

I wheeze. I am a good wheezer. It is a great feeling to discover gifts you never knew you had.

"Please . . ." he says. "Stop making fun of my asthma."

He breathes rapidly four or five times.

So do I.

"Are you having an asthma attack?" I ask.

He nods. He looks at me and puts his hand out for his bag. I throw it hard at him. The bag lands on his chest. There is a gasp from one of the girls.

"Don't worry," I turn around and say. "It will make his chest strong. He needs a strong chest."

I think of the girls in the class. What strong chests they have.

Viren is a thin boy, but his chest expands like a wrestler's. I push the bag harder against him.

"Please," he says. "I want to go home."

I open his bag and take out a notebook. It is labelled *Moral Science*. Maybe I should keep it for myself. Viren is physically weak, but morally strong.

"Please. My mummy is coming." His voice cracks.

I wait for the class to laugh, and they do. A tear gathers in the corner of Viren's right eye. Now there are two. He tries hard to breathe and control his tears. They stream.

"Who is your mummy coming with?" I ask.

"No one," he cries.

"You liar," I say. "She's coming with Shakespeare!"

I am surprised that no one laughs. Miss Bardet does not find it funny either. She just stands in the doorway and looks at a thin boy, pretty blue bag stuck to his chest, crying for air.

The taxi halts outside Lucky Moon. Each morning before school, while my friends had tea and buttered bread, I drank sugarcane juice at Lucky Moon. After I got typhoid, I switched to tea. I used the tea as a dip for bun-maska. The owner always sat at the counter, head a little bent, dispensing change at the pace of a bank teller. He would shout out the order from his counter to the waiter in the back.

I take my little brown package and climb the three white steps that lead to the tables. The sugarcane juice machine is still there, battered and dirty, with the required quota of flies and mosquitoes circling its periphery. The tables are the same: three wooden legs and a round top of white marble. The chairs are wooden with elegant backs, reminiscent of the English. The owner, Irani Uncle as we used to call him, is not at the counter. I sit at the table with my back to the man who has taken his place. I face the kitchen. It has the same grime-covered walls from years ago.

I do not like the waiter's walk. He has been watching too many Hindi movies. His rag is too clean. This means he does not wipe the bread crumbs and spilt tea off the table.

"Chai-paani?" he asks.

"Cutting la," I tell him.

I love the word "cutting." We all did in school. It means nothing more than a cup of tea, three-fourths full, but it is all in the name. Students who did not use it were considered unversed in the ways of men. It is like saying, "I would like a cup of tea, please," as opposed to, "Get me some tea, you bastard." When you are young, there is nothing more horrible than being cultured. Low class was in, and we had plenty of it.

The waiter comes with one cutting. He puts it on my table, spilling a little. "Anything else?" he asks, irritated.

He is obviously an amateur. Deliberation by the customer is a necessity at Lucky Moon. A good waiter knows that. In fact, I made a mistake. I did not follow protocol. When you enter, you should look around as though you own the place and, with an air of disdain, select the table you wish to sit at as though you are doing the owner a favor by gracing Lucky Moon. Then you remove the pack of Charminar, Gold Flake or 555 from the left pocket of your white shirt (it has to be a white shirt) and place the pack on the table as though no one else in the country can afford cigarettes. When you know for certain that someone is watching you, you remove a cigarette from the pack. Tap it twice, only twice, on the tabletop. (One tap suggests you do not know what you are doing, and three taps or more suggests you are copying the actions of someone else.) The waiter arrives, and if he is sensible he will not speak. He will observe, wait upon you, as you put the cigarette to your lips, light it with a match and stare at the flame as it pulls away. You blow out smoke as if it is your gift to this earth. Then you lean back against the chair. Only then — *only then* — may the waiter ask for your order. And even though you have the same item every day, you deliberate.

Today I did not deliberate. I am ashamed of myself. I will make up for it by wasting the waiter's time.

"Anything else?" he asks.

I deliberate. I have mastered the art of deliberation through years of schooling. I look at the glass showcase near the entrance. Colgate toothpaste, Parachute oil, Hamam soap, all the splendors of the modern world are displayed before me. I notice that the waiter is getting impatient. So I lean back on my chair and look at his face. I do not look directly into his eyes, but at his nose and ears, so that he gets uncomfortable. He starts shifting. I clear my throat as if I am about to deliver a speech before Parliament.

"Bun-maska la," I say.

"Just one?"

"Let me think," I say. I put the only hand I have to my chin. My school friends would be proud of me. I miss them. "One," I tell the waiter. To me, it is important to be low class.

I look outside and see a few parked cars. All old Fiats. Is no one rich anymore? I used to come in a bloody Mercedes. But then, my parents never loved me. So it was a fine balance. I used to water the tires of the Mercedes with my friends. Let us paint the tires yellow, I would say, but no hands. So we would all put our hands in the air and spray. My driver would be most upset. I will tell Daddy, he would shout. But it's not *your* daddy's car, I would reply. Then our spray painting would go all wrong because we would break out into peals of laughter. Those were the days of a privileged existence.

The sweet buttered bun I ordered soon arrives on a small steel plate. I can detect the waiter's finger smudges on the surface of the plate. There is very little butter on the bread; it is more a thin film than a coating. The cutting is still hot. I blow into it before my first sip. The sugarcane machine has started. The flies and mosquitoes have grown accustomed to its clumsy rotations as it spits out crushed shoots of cane. I eat the bun-maska without dipping it in the cutting. The waiter is in the back boiling some more chai. I call out to him with The Kiss.

The Kiss is an unsentimental gesture in this case. A man's lips purse to produce a sucking sound. The result is a universally accepted means of beckoning. But The Kiss cannot be used to call women. Bus conductors, drivers, beggars and friends respond well to it. If you call a woman that way, then her handbag will slap your face.

The waiter responds to my kiss but not too kindly — his Hindi movie walk commences. I place my handy brown bag on the white tabletop.

"Waiter!" I say defiantly. "There's a fly in my soup." My transition from low class to highbrow is sudden, but the situation demands it.

"What?"

"Did you not hear me? There's a fly in my soup."

"This is not soup."

"It tastes like soup. What sort of cutting is this?"

"Lucky Moon cutting. Best in Clear Road."

"What do we do about the fly?"

"Where is the fly?" He bends forward to inspect the cutting.

"It flew," I say.

"Boss, this area no fool around."

"Okay, I will finish this soup even though it is contaminated. You will be responsible for giving a cripple jaundice."

"Cripple?"

"You mean you did not notice my deformity? Manager! Who is your manager?"

"I not see . . ."

"A complete lack of service. Absence of the human element!"

By now, he has no clue what I am saying. So to give him a visual stimulant, I remove the finger from the bag. In this setting it looks edible. The man moves away from the table.

"What is that?"

"I will dip it in my cutting."

"Cannot eat!" He staggers back some more. There is no trace of the Hindi movie walk now.

"You want to try?"

"Abdul bhai! Abdul bhai!" he shouts hysterically. I assume Abdul bhai is the owner. I must be careful. Abdul bhai sounds like dynamite.

Abdul gets up from his place behind the counter and hitches up his black pants. He grunts a little. I had mistaken his hair to be oily. It looks more like water. That is not a good sign. People who water their hair are dangerous. For one, it shows they have too much free time and will therefore snap at the slightest provocation. Two, the hair-watering type is commonly of a certain profile, mainly gangly (belonging to a gang). Three, the constant need for wetness is the result of a hot head.

"Abdul bhai," the waiter starts again. "This man is being shyana."

"I'm not being clever," I tell Abdul.

"Shyana buntai?" Abdul's hand is the size of my foot. I thank God for my deformity; it might inspire pity in Abdul.

"Abdul bhai," I say. I turn to my left so that the absence of my arm is even more apparent.

"I am not Abdul bhai," he says.

"You are not?" I ask.

"I am."

"I am confused."

"I am, but not to you."

"Sorry," I tell him.

I slowly drag the finger toward the edge of the table. A few more inches and I can place it in the bag. I must not lose the finger at all costs.

"AK Munna Tiger Lily!" he shouts.

"What?"

"You must call me AK Munna Tiger Lily."

"Okay," I say. By now, the waiter has calmed down. His eyes are on the finger, so I stop moving it.

"Go on," Abdul says. "Call me by my name."

"Could you repeat it, please?"

He steps a foot closer.

"Sir, I wish to get your name perfectly right," I plead.

"AK Munna Tiger Lily."

"A gun, a boy, a tiger, a lily," I say to myself.

"A gun? You have a gun?" asks Abdul.

"No. I'm just being literal. AK for 47. It will help me remember your name. And Munna means boy. So."

"So you don't have a gun?"

"I don't have an arm to carry a gun, AK Munna Tiger Lily," I say.

"I noticed," he replies.

"What a relief. This waiter did not even see that I'm a cripple. AK Munna Tiger Lily, you are a pride to the hotel industry. Did you train in Switzerland?"

"Without training," he says proudly.

"That's remarkable," I say. "If only this man here had your manners."

Abdul looks at the waiter. "How many times I have told you to be courteous?"

"Courteous?" replies the waiter.

This is my chance. I must point out this show of disrespect on the waiter's part. "Sir AK, this man is making a fool of your courtesy."

"Are you?" he asks the waiter, who fidgets nervously with his rag.

"Abdul bhai, do not listen to him," pleads the waiter.

"AK Munna Tiger Lily!" he booms.

"But I always call you Abdul bhai."

"You have lost that privilege."

I add: "I think Sir AK is much better. It is regal."

Adbul raises an eyebrow. "Yes, it is much more better."

"But this man wants to eat a finger," shouts the waiter.

I put the finger in the brown paper bag and get up from my table. Abdul puts his hand on my shoulder.

"You're not going anywhere," he says.

I remove the finger from the bag. "Let me go or I will eat this finger right in front of you," I threaten.

Abdul takes his hand off my shoulder. The waiter moves away as well. I put the finger two inches away from my mouth. I try not to let my revulsion show.

"Okay, leave," says Abdul.

"That's not all," I say. "I want you to tell me where this finger points."

"Where it points?"

"Don't pretend," I say. "You know the In-charge. You know Baba Rakhu. Quick, where does it point? I warn you, I'm getting hungry."

"I told you he is crazy!" shouts the waiter.

"Sir AK! Sir AK! Sir AK!" Abdul yells back.

"I will eat this biscuit."

"Wait," says Abdul. "If you take a lotus and place it on water, what will happen?"

"It will float," I reply.

"Wrong! It will sink."

"Why?"

"The giant who lives underwater will pull it from below."

"What giant?"

The finger is perilously close to my mouth. I am speaking into it as if it is a microphone.

"This giant, is it a hint?" I ask. At this point I would look for clues in the cornea of the blind. But I have faith that I will be directed to the next point from here. When I was young, all my learning took place at Lucky Moon.

Abdul looks at his slab of a hand and steps forward to hit me. As I retreat, my foot lands on a shoot of crushed sugarcane.

"Tell me what to do with the finger!" I plead.

"Get rid of it. It reeks of death," he says.

I nod in the direction of the flies, mosquitoes and crushed cane, and step out of Lucky Moon. I am glad time has not made it sanitary; I may even organize a school reunion here. Naturally, I will invite only those who used the word "cutting." I look at the street and notice that apart from two handcarts and an old scooter, Clare Road is still Clear.

THE GIANT WHO LIVED UNDERWATER

Here is the story of Gardulla that I had heard as a child, about how he came to live underwater. Let him be known as Gardulla the Giant. Let his home be the river Baya in an ancient land. Let it be written in blood that Gardulla the Giant was as real as the mosques of this city. Let him be an awning that protects us from the dark clouds of jealousy, for it was jealousy that brought about his birth and ultimately his demise.

Long before Gardulla was born, the river Baya had a friend, a peacock that walked along her banks. The two enjoyed racing with each other. Baya was a young river then, fast and gushing, but she did not always win. The peacock had a red and blue fan that reached far into the sky when open. When the wind blew strong, it carried the peacock with a speed that Baya could only wish for.

It was only natural, then, that the two became lovers. It was natural, but accidental as well. Very early one morning, when it was still dark, the peacock woke to practice his run. It was the month when the mountains ate the wind. As such, he had been losing to Baya of late and she did not let him forget it. "Your fan has no wind," she would taunt. "Maybe you should keep it closed forever."

The peacock would pretend to enjoy the banter, but would bow his head in shame as soon as Baya flowed past. He needed a victory to make Baya's mouth dry of hurtful words.

As the peacock raced at the foot of Baya, he thought he heard a wind. He stopped to open his fan. It had been days since he had felt the wind and he wanted to remind himself what victory tasted like. As he waited, he knew his eyes would soon close with that first rush of air, the blue of his feathers trapping the wind, storing it for future use.

But the wind came from another direction, for the first time ever, with such great force that he was plunged into the river. He had never touched Baya before, and to fall upon her, like some cheap rock, brought him great shame. Even greater shame than when he lost his races.

Baya liked the warmth of the peacock's feathers, the melting of his colors with her liquid skin. She slowed down and raised him to her mouth in the darkness. She kept him there, swirled around him, until she seeped into his every pore. The peacock put his head inside her and drank her. In this manner, they carried each other in themselves until the darkness lifted. As the first drops of light fell, the peacock opened. Balanced on Baya, the fringes of his blue and red fan glowed as the sun rose behind him. The two stopped racing forever; instead they vowed to carry each other to heaven.

For giants to be born, a special seed must be sown. Or a tangle of weeds must come loose on their own. Giants are special, like secret recipes. They are not born *by* or *of*. They are born *because*.

After the racing stopped, Baya and the peacock were entwined, it seemed forever. Wherever Baya went, the peacock followed. He loved how long her reach was, how she would sometimes rise from behind him, and, at other times come toward him in a playful rage. Their world was complete and each day, as the darkness left, the peacock would dip his head into Baya and let her enter him.

But there are some days when the sun does not rise. Or even if it does, the darkness is so thick you cannot see it. When such darkness comes, your eyes record a false light, one that you have created out of fear. On one such day, Baya expressed her dread. She grew cold, even though the peacock tried hard to keep her warm. His skin was not enough, so he bent down low into her belly to take her in. He had never gone so deep before, and Baya thought it was someone else — another lover. Like a fool, she called this other lover's name.

The peacock felt a burning in his heart. It grew so strong that Baya tried to move away from him. This time, the peacock needed no wind. His heart drove him to tearful rage and he rose up out of Baya and followed her, his fan, black as a bad dream, spun over the sky in evil might. The closer he came to her, the farther away Baya went. They raced, gathering speed with every drop of hate and fear. As the peacock's heat grew, Baya tried harder to escape. She flung herself far and wide, much farther than she knew, and finally lashed the peacock against a tree.

Blue and red filled the air. Before Baya could regain her calm, the song of the peacock's death began. It cut through her center and she parted. She took over land that was not hers. She took over flowers and grass and herbs and small fruit trees. It was not her fault, but she could not stop her grieving. Finally, unable to bear the sight of the peacock fallen, she swallowed him whole and hid him in the folds of her skin.

A vow had been broken. Baya and the peacock had promised each other heaven and gave each other death instead. But they gave each other something else, too: a special seed that the peacock's death had left behind. Because the peacock had been jealous, Gardulla was born. Thus, he was born not *by* or *of*, he was born *because*. The wind chanted his name like a favorite season. "Gardulla," said the wind. And Gardulla popped his little head out of the water and got his first taste of the sun. The wind, unable to see his feet, thought that the little boy was tall enough to stand on his mother's bed. "Why," said the wind, "is this Gardulla a giant?" And for a second time, he was born *because* — because the wind could not see.

It is absurd that a river and a peacock could give birth to a little boy. It is absurd that upon being told by the wind that he was a giant, Gardulla simply stretched his legs out and became one. By the same token, I ask you, why is the wind allowed to talk? We cannot see it, but we listen to it more clearly than to the words of men. And why is it that while *we* are made of water, only the clouds can give it to us? We could be trees. Or we could be alive only because trees breathe us in.

Gardulla could never leave the water. He thought of Baya as water and not as his mother, because she was too distant. Although she lay against him all the time, not once did she coil around him. She was cold and silent and Gardulla did not know why. His only joy was watching the world around him. By now Baya had stopped crying and had shrunk to her old size once more. The grass, flowers, herbs and fruit trees grew along her banks again.

Time passed in this manner. Days repeated themselves with such monotony that new days were a thing long forgotten. Until a little girl, her hair brown as a haystack, came to play alongside Baya. Baya liked the little girl; whenever the little girl came, Baya sang. At first Gardulla thought nothing of this. But then he felt the warmth of his mother, and he knew it was not for him. The warmth reached toward the little girl — it changed its path like a treacherous arrow. Unable to bear the sight of the little girl, Gardulla put his head inside the water for the first time.

He was horrified by what he saw. Feathers of blue and red were scattered across the folds of his mother's skin. When Baya sensed that Gardulla saw the peacock, she tried to hide his feathers. And when you hide something, it means your heart is halved. The other half is buried under your lips.

The next time the little girl came to play, Gardulla's eyes shot blood. But he lowered them so she would not see his anger. The little girl ran through the grass and became thirsty. She bent toward Baya to quench her thirst. Baya could not help it. She felt warm again. The little girl reminded Baya of her lover. Gardulla, on the other hand, was like a carving on a tombstone for Baya, synonymous with her husband's death. Gardulla was a record of all that she wished to forget.

Now Gardulla was sure. The girl was his stepsister and his mother's favorite. As the little girl drank, he reached his arm out and caught her. When he lifted the little girl, Baya became fast and young again. She raged against him with all her might. She crushed him, telling him that she was killing him with the force of her love. Gardulla's life poured out of his eyes. He could not believe Baya was doing this, and yet it made no difference. He could have fought back, but he simply let go of the little girl. In time, the force of Baya crushed his head. Not wishing to keep him close, she sent him to her feet, where he was taken away by the earth.

There are always flowers for the dead. Baya placed a white lotus in the large palm of her dead son. The lotus sank with Gardulla. Thus, whenever you see a sinking lotus, it is because the giant who lives underwater pulls it down from below.

LOVE LANE

So here I am in Love Lane ready to mourn the death of lovers. It is hot and I am worried that the finger I carry will melt. I must find its use fast. It will come to me like rain when I least expect it.

I walked this road many times as a boy, from Lucky Moon to Love Lane. It is a ten-minute walk. During those ten minutes, I would think of how eating dinner at home would make me sick. The silence between Mother and Father as they let the clink and scratch of forks and spoons speak instead of their own voices, the razor cuts on Father's face increasing as their love decreased, while I stared at the mangoes on the table, the fish, the bread, how it all was cut up and open, just like Father.

During the ten-minute walk, I also thought of never going home again. What if I kept on walking? I would cross the outer limits of the city, then the suburbs, the towns, the villages, until I would stand before a vast expanse of water. A large white bird would pick me up, fly me to the land of my choice, and I would ask it to go where everyone is always talking, where boys play cricket and girls have pretty brown hair, and where mothers do not sleep with supreme court judges and fathers have no razor marks on their faces.

But I never saw a large white bird. There were only sparrows picking on crumbs that beggars had left behind. So I would go back to Lucky Moon, where my worried driver would be searching for me. He would cage me in my black Mercedes and take me home just in time for the silence of dinner.

This road is called Love Lane for a reason. When you walk through it, you ignore the loud noise of schoolgirls. You do not hear the religious discourse of the old man with a long beard who is spitting wisdom into a megaphone. The month-old puddle from the leaking sewage pipe does not affect you. You ignore the swarm of flies that fuss over it like women. For when two hands meet in Love Lane, they can make deserts wet.

Today I see another breed of lovers. They are seated on wooden chairs under a long white canopy, staring at the bearded wise man. They are lovers of religion. If the lovers of the flesh are absent, these will do. The wise man speaks to at least forty people, all of whom hang on his every word as if he is the world's next prophet. He holds the megaphone to his lips with his right hand, and directs world prosperity with the other.

"Even kings take help from beggars," he shouts. "So why not you?"

The canopy is hung outside an all girls' school. By the time the girls grow up to be women, they shall be pure and helpful. There is nothing like religion for breakfast, lunch and dinner.

"So why not you?" repeats the wise man.

No one answers. It would be disrespectful to do so.

"I will tell you why," he says.

By the manner in which they shake their heads, I can tell a few of the listeners are already ashamed.

"You are too proud to ask for God's help," he says. "Too proud."

There are three women seated in the last row. They could not agree more. They would cook for this wise man; such is their awe for the saver of us all.

"The mountain will not come to you," he says. "You must walk to it."

A man wearing a white bush shirt and black trousers has fallen asleep in the first row.

"Look at this man!" shouts the wise one. "He does not even have the manners to listen to the word of God."

If God had one word to tell us, what would it be? He has created too much for one word to explain.

"You know what this man is?" asks the prophet.

Once more, they do not answer because they are not meant to.

"This man is proud," he shouts. "Pride is what allowed the evil spirit to conquer good."

I think the poor man is simply asleep. He is probably trying to rest after a hot afternoon of fixing a telephone line or selling combs out of a torn suitcase.

"This man is a peacock!" says the old man. "Too proud!"

For once, I must admit, religion has saved me.

In this world there is no such thing as coincidence. Hospitals are real and jails are real. Believing in chance is like saying the opening of flowers happens by mistake. If there is a peacock here, a river and a giant are close by.

The wise man takes his megaphone close to the sleeping peacock. "God wants us all to rise!" he shouts.

Everyone slowly gets up from their chairs. The creak of their backs indicates that this has been one long afternoon of enlightenment.

The man still sleeps. It is quite superb.

The wise man will not tolerate defiance. After all, he is not selling onions at a high price. His claims cannot be dismissed with such apathy. He is offering the Fruit of God. It is free, but can cost us the universe if we do not eat it.

"We must not only get up from our seats," he says. "We must rise as human beings!"

The man's sleep breaks. Maybe he has sold his last comb or there are no more telephone wires to be fixed. Everyone looks at him. His eyes have the red blur of sleep and confusion. He looks at his arms, which are already folded. All he has to do is stand up and he is a gentleman again.

"I fear for your soul," says the wise man. "We all fear for his soul," he adds. He looks at the others, who are thankful that they slept well at home and did not doze off during the wise man's edict.

"Brothers, don't we fear for his soul?" he asks. "We must teach him a lesson. God wants it so."

The waking man's hands are not folded anymore. They are by his side as he looks around at the faces. They are young and old, but mostly old. The young seek religion only after they have collected enough sin. Ask me; I know. The crowd starts moving toward the man who was asleep. In a second faster than light, the man runs.

Brown paper bag in hand, I bolt after him. He is my racing peacock. I look for rivers on either side of the street. There are bullock carts trudging along, cycles lined against the side wall of a ration shop, and a circle of men in white shirts smoking cigarettes during their tea break.

The peacock does not stop running. He darts through a taxi and a handcart and enters a small passage that separates two buildings. I must not lose my peacock. Try running without an arm. It is a circus act. It is like stirring soup without a ladle.

Residents of both buildings are outside. One man brushes his teeth, perched like an eagle on his outside landing. A woman beats her yellow sari with a wet cloth again and again as if she is lashing a woman who hides inside. She sees the peacock rush past. Then she sees me.

"Thief!" she shouts. "Stop that thief!"

I am not sure who she thinks the thief is. I am the chaser, but then again I am carrying a brown paper packet in my hand. The peacock is empty-handed.

A short man leaning against huge drums of water decides to be heroic. It is *his* little lane, and he will be talked about in the days to come. So he puffs and heaves and overturns a drum. Water gushes out. It is not the least bit dangerous, but the runner stops.

The sari-lasher has come up behind me with the tooth-brusher. The tooth-brusher tries to speak and spits black paste onto me instead.

"What did he steal?" asks the sari-lasher.

"I . . . nothing," I say.

"Stop that man!" she shouts.

But the man is not going anywhere. He walks toward us, his chest heaving. The water from the drum seeps through my sandals and wets my feet. It feels dirty, as though truckloads of children with runny noses have bathed in it.

"He is not . . . a thief," I say.

"Not a chor?" asks the tooth-brusher. "Then why were you following him?"

"I was not following," I say.

"What, you were exercising?" he snaps. "Tell the truth, cripple. Why you were following?"

"I was following him to return this bag."

The peacock looks at the brown paper bag in my hand.

"You must have left it inside God's tent," I say. I extend the bag toward the peacock. The water has soaked my feet now and rushes past on a downward slope.

"It's not mine," he says. "I had to meet my wife half an hour ago. I'm late. That's why I was running."

You were running from God, so you could get to your wife. Woman is truly powerful.

"I have to go," he says.

The drum-turner, the sari-lasher and the tooth-brusher are most disappointed that no confrontation will take place. So I try.

"But you might know what to do with it," I ask.

"What do you mean?"

I feel something nibbling against my foot. I know what it is, but I refuse to look down. I simply stare at the peacock.

"Do with what?" he asks.

"This bag," I reply.

A small rat is feasting on my toes. I try to stamp on it but it escapes. In the water, it is a black prune running.

"Saala rat," says the drum-turner. "This gully has too many rats. I'll show them."

Perhaps he says this because his bravery did not pay off. No thief was caught and he will not be talked about in the days to come. "I will drown all those rats," he says.

He walks to a drum and empties it in our direction. Dried flowers that must have been part of a garland wash past me.

"Ay!" shouts the sari-lasher. "Don't waste water!"

"Saala rats!" he shouts.

He overturns a third drum. It is the last one. Empty cigarette packs, matchboxes, torn balloons and two more rats come toward me. The water rushes past like a river.

"My wife!" says the peacock with the suddenness of a traffic signal coming on.

He flees from strife, toward his wife, where he will beg for his life for being late. The water follows him, curling at his feet. In that moment, I know I must start running again. Love and history are repeating themselves for me. The peacock is racing with the river. I see the river part as it breaks into two thin streams.

FLAME AND FORTUNE

Will the peacock be lashed against a tree after slipping? Will his wife push him into oncoming traffic for being late? It does not concern me. I was never after the peacock. I want the giant. As the river forks into Love Lane again, I stand and survey the street. In front of me there is a shop that sells cooking utensils. Next to it is a cycle shop. At one time these cycles were parrot green, ink blue and sun orange. Now they look a beaten-down black. Cycling. One more thing I cannot do. So I look at the cars that trickle past. Driving. One more thing I cannot do.

I think of one-armed gems: stabbing with a knife, using a gun, picking flowers, snapping your fingers, waving goodbye. There is a place in this world for cripples. We cannot ride cycles, we cannot drive cars, but we can kill. It is hard to swallow the fact that I failed at suicide. If I had succeeded, I would not be staring at this large man reading a young girl's palm near the cycle shop.

I have found my giant. Yes, it has been too easy. But this only means that what lies ahead will be disastrous.

I quickly cross the street toward the giant, but in my haste I drop the brown paper bag. I raise both my arms to the skies to stop the oncoming black Fiat from crushing it. There is no harm in me thinking that I have raised *two* arms. In my mind I have raised two arms and it is the thought that counts.

The driver curses me. (I am told to fetch my sister so that he can make her swelter and welter like the she-dog she is.) I pick my bag up and approach this large man who reads the palm of the young girl.

"Let's go," says the young girl's lover. He tugs at her skirt. He does not want her palm to be read.

"But Suresh," says the girl. "I want to hear what more this man has to say."

"But he's saying such bad things about us."

"What if they are such-mooch? Suresh, give him money."

"But . . ."

"If you love me, you'll pay for my fortune."

"I *am* paying a fortune," says Suresh.

"You call twenty rupees a fortune?"

"See, I'm right," says the giant. "Your match is not good."

Suresh unhappily plucks out twenty rupees from his shirt pocket. With irritation, he thrusts them into the girl's palm. I like the shirt Suresh wears. It is so loud, even car horns will sound like whispers.

"Here's the money. Tell me what the stars say about me," says the young girl.

"I will," says the giant. "But I must do something before that." He looks at me. "Is this some balcony show? What are you looking at?"

"I also want to know my future," I say. "After her."

He does not say anything. He takes the girl's money and her hand in his. Her hand looks tiny in comparison, like a doll's. He rubs his palm onto hers and slips his tongue out and in. He takes his time feeling the young girl. I glance at her face and there is no doubt that Suresh is a lucky man. She has been freshly plucked from a tree. How can she allow him to wear that shirt? It makes a circus tent look like a hospital sheet.

Suresh grits his teeth together. "Now he's touching you. I cannot bear it!"

"How you think so vulgar, Suresh! Like a mavali," she says.

"I'm the mavali? I'm the mavali?" shouts Suresh.

"Your future is good," says the giant.

"See?" she tells Suresh. "You were worried."

"But only on your own," he continues.

"Why?"

"A possessive lover will deny you your dream," he says.

"Enough!" says Suresh. "Let's leave."

"What dream?" asks the girl.

"Your dream of becoming a heroine."

"How you knew?"

Even I knew. With a face like that, what else could her brain want?

"See this line?" says the giant. "That is your dream line. It is getting cut again and again by your love line. It means the one you love will cut your dreams."

"Suresh," she says. "Is this true?"

Suresh is climbing the roofs of the city and is ready to jump off. Suresh is having such bad thoughts about the giant that even a crow will turn white.

"I cannot believe you are so stupid!" Suresh tells her.

Suresh has just jumped off the roof and dug himself a deep hole.

"What did you say?"

"I did not mean it, darling," says Suresh.

"You called me stupid," she says. "And you have before also made fun of my movie dreams."

"I love you. You will be a big star, I promise."

Men lie like Tuesdays that say they are Sundays. We do not deserve women.

"You're just saying that," she says. I detect tears.

"Don't cry, my jaan," says Suresh. "I did not mean to . . ."

Then he makes a mistake. He holds her.

Never touch a lover during an argument. You are a serpent to her, not a lovable rabbit. Remember that, you fool.

"Don't touch me!" She walks away.

"But my lotus . . ." Suresh follows her.

I am definitely on track. He called her a lotus. This man *is* my giant.

The young girl will leave Suresh. She has movie dreams and so she will walk alone. I imagine that along the way her legs will spread like cheap butter, her breasts will come out as often as moons do, sheets will crumple, and the scent of paisa will fill her heart, especially those parts left empty by Suresh.

"Please read my hand," I tell the giant.

"Cross your legs and sit down," he says.

I sit on the footpath. Ants circle a packet of half-eaten sweet bhel on the ground. I place my brown bag next to it.

"First, I need a hit," he says.

"Hit?"

From behind his back, he removes a whiskey bottle. It is empty. Without looking, he puts it to his lips. When nothing enters his mouth, he pulls the bottle away.

"It's empty," he says. "Totally useless."

He throws the bottle at me.

Once again I am forced to catch a whiskey bottle in my right hand. Once again the sleeping bird from my past will awaken, trudge up a black tree, and yell.

#

It is English class.

I sit next to Viren. I hate English. I do not even know Shakespeare and yet I am afraid of him. Viren is not. They are best friends. He has written Shakespeare's name under the lid of his desk.

Miss Moses dabs her neck with a white handkerchief. She does not like me. I asked her once why she sweats so much. Her reply was that she does not sweat, she *perspires*. There is a huge difference. Pigs sweat, ladies perspire.

The fans in class do not work. The electricity has gone off today, so Miss Moses is very wet. Three of the windowpanes are broken; it means extra air will enter. Even though the fans are not working, we are not allowed to open the rest of the windows. Miss Moses does not think it proper. Ladies do not open windows.

"Viren," says Miss Moses. She calls his name very clearly, as if he is a diamond or something. Viren stands up. He always stands up when teachers talk to him. The teachers love him for it. He is *so* respectful.

"Yes, Miss Moses," he answers in a soft voice.

"I want you to take a bow."

Viren coyly lowers his head and smiles. The teachers love him for this. He is *so* humble.

"Go ahead," she says. "Your essay got the highest mark in the class."

Moses bows. Viren might as well be called Moses. He is *so* holy.

"Thank you, Miss Moses," says Viren.

If they do not stop soon, I will be sick. They should shine apples for each other.

"There's another essay that deserves special mention," says Miss Moses.

Good. Now there are two students who can shine apples for Miss Moses. She will need two apples. An apple a day keeps the doctor away. But if there are too many apples, one has to consider the cooks and the broth they spoil. I am quite intelligent. But no one in the class knows this. It truly upsets me that someone of my genius lies undetected. I look up at the fans. They are as still as men at funerals.

"There's another essay that stands out," she says. "It's only natural that this essay got the *lowest* mark because the person who wrote it is busy staring at fans."

Viren looks at me and laughs. The class also laughs. Miss Moses does not like laughter, but this time she will allow it because she dislikes me more than she dislikes laughter.

"Can you tell us why you're staring at the fan?" she asks me.

"He wants to be a fan bearer," says Viren.

The class loves it. I let out a weak smile. Viren opens the lid of his desk and lowers his head so Miss Moses cannot see him.

"You came last," he says softly. "But it's not your fault. You come from a long line of donkeys."

"Shakespeare is a donkey," I reply.

But it is weak, so weak. It is very hot, so hot that even the fans feel it. Miss Moses says something but I do not hear her. I look at Viren, at that thin neck of his, and wonder where he got the courage to be so bold. I must stay calm. I must wait till school is over.

"You don't even know who Shakespeare is," whispers Viren.

"I do," I say.

"You can't even spell his name."

"I can."

"Do it."

I look at the fans and they are still not working. I do not know where to look.

"Fan bearer," says Viren. "The answer will not come from heaven."

For once I wish it would. I am even willing to pray.

"I knew it," he says. "Your father is a donkey."

I rise out of my chair and bang the desk lid down on him. The class goes silent. Miss Moses yells. I look around at all their faces. I suddenly realize that I do not like any of them. They are just like family.

And then I do it again. I hold Viren's neck so he cannot move and bring the heavy lid down. Miss Moses gets up from her chair. There is a loud scream from Viren. It surprises me and I let go of his neck. He does not move his head. I try to get the desk lid off him but it will not move. It is stuck to his head. I jerk again until I see the blood. There is a nail in his eye. Our schools should have safer desks.

❧

I put the empty whiskey bottle back on the ground. The ants are enjoying the bhel. Soon they will eat my brown paper bag. Even though it is only early evening, the sky has suddenly darkened. It happens a lot in this city. The sky forgets that it is blue. It sees the dusty winding streets, the naked children, the withered dogs, the widows, the drug-selling temples, and it turns sad. It takes away its own light in shame.

"What happened?" asks the giant. "You don't like whiskey?"

"No," I say.

"Something from the past?"

"Forget the past," I say. "I want my future."

"Give me your hand."

I show him my right palm.

"No," he says. "Show me your left hand."

"But it's not there."

"Just like your past."

"What do you mean?"

"Your past does not exist. You don't want it to."

"Yes," I say. "I have lost my arm. I wish to forget that."

"Think back," he says. "Before you lost the arm."

"I don't want to," I say.

"Take it out," he says.

"What?"

"Take out what's in the bag."

"How do you know something is in the bag?"

"You stopped traffic for it," he says. "Must be worth a lot."

I lift the bag and wipe off the few ants that are on it. I remove the dark finger and place it in his palm. It does not surprise him at all. It is as if I have placed a ballpoint pen in his hand, or an incense stick, or a dark candle.

"You are doing everything opposite," he says. "See how you have placed it?"

He turns the finger around in his palm until it points my way.

"You must go there," he says.

"Where?"

"Where the finger points. To your heart."

"My heart?"

"Everything lies there."

I look at the finger and suddenly understand what he is saying. We circle around people and look at backs of heads, collars, buttons, sleeves, folds of trousers. But when finally the heart is revealed, we turn away and tie our shoelaces. From the very beginning, the finger was pointed at me.

THE LOST ARM

If the heart must speak, then the heart must travel backwards, two months, to a hospital bed.

The ceiling fan moved very slowly so I could count how many blades it had. Three fat, rusty blades. It cut air clumsily and made a strange sound — *wong wong wong* — as it circled above me, as though it were mourning the death of a drowning victim in the Indo-China Sea. Perhaps hospital fans keep a record of each patient below them. So the person before me, on those cold sheets, must have been Chinese.

I looked outside and it was night. The lights in the sky were not stars. They were the eyes of dead people shining, blinking, calling out, and hoping that I'd come to them soon. I was walking through the dark temper of trees, speaking the murmur of some other man's heart. I was outgrowing the trees and grass, but growing downward, like wells, like people who are always sorry.

I needed to sit to get some clarity. I propped myself up on my elbows. A sick feeling invaded me.

I had just one elbow.

I lifted my right hand and reached across toward my left. I did this slowly. Then I drew my hand away. I was in no hurry to confirm anything. Parts of the walls shone as car headlights fell upon them and died.

That was the first time I saw the flying cockroaches. Instead of closing my eyes, I wanted to let them in. They fluttered like brown butterflies, growing large, then small, and large again. They sat before me in a row on the bedpost, priests keeping guard, praying with the whirring of wings, driving *something* away. I looked up and the fan had stopped circling. I heard a dog barking as if he had spotted something. Then the dog grew quiet.

All at once the cockroaches stopped praying. The bedpost rattled and the cockroaches shook, stripped of their priesthood. They turned into scared little children. Tiny holes appeared in the window, which were soon filled with black. Not the black of night, but a darker, more truthful black. The color belonged to the black cockroaches. They tore at the brown ones, devoured them as if feasting on charred pieces of meat. One by one, the brown fell to the floor. When the last one fell, the black took their place on the bedpost.

They willed my right arm to rise. Even though I did not want it to, my arm reached across to my left side and touched the surface of the bed. I felt the cold of a white bedsheet. I tried to pull my arm away but it kept going higher. The black ones bowed their heads. When I touched my stump, they flew out the tiny holes in the window into the clear night sky.

I lay in bed knowing there had to have been a mistake. Only beggars and poor children lose their arms. There is not enough food in their bodies and the heart is unable to send blood everywhere. The limbs anticipate this and fall off on purpose. My arm must be under the bed, I reasoned. I tried to get up but my head stayed down. The orderly must have taken the arm to clean. Who had brought me here, and which hospital was I in? A dam had burst and the questions came like burning hot water.

When the orderly arrived the next morning, I kept silent. He had the answers and I did not wish to hear them. So I let him turn me around and do his job. Was I in an animal hospital? Outside, rabbits played in the grass. Some lay sick on their backs, calling out for help; others put their soft heads together and prayed for the sick ones to be well again. The dog who had barked the night before circled outside my window. He kept looking at the sky. Sick rabbits crawled from under his legs and came out well. The orderly left and as the door closed, all the lights went out and I slept again.

At some point, I remember telling the orderly that I was cold even though I was not. Even though they had turned the fan off, I kept asking for extra blankets. The orderly replied that I was already using two blankets. But I insisted I was cold. Only a shawl could keep me warm, I said. So he brought me a shawl. Cover my head, I said. So he covered my head with the shawl and I slept again. In truth, I wanted the shawl for when I left. They were mad if they thought I was going to walk out without a shawl that covered what I had lost.

When I woke, the orderly was still there. Or perhaps he had just walked in. He stared at me and pity poured out of his eyes, enough to fill large vats. I asked him how I had lost my arm. He told me he had smoked twenty beedis the night I was brought to the hospital. I arrived when he went down to smoke his twenty-first, in the back of the hospital where the garbage is stored, where the orderlies meet to smoke during their breaks. He was the only one there. He could not remember if the moon was out. I told him I did not care much for the moon. Just as he had lit a match to light his twenty-first beedi, a Mahindra jeep had rushed toward him. He lit his beedi anyway. As he took his first dum, the vehicle stopped right in front of him. A door opened, a body fell out of the backseat, rolled onto the street and settled at the foot of a huge garbage container. That was *you*, he said. I thought so, I replied. Did I have my arm? He did not remember if he threw the beedi to the floor or if it just fell from his mouth, but I *did* have an arm. It could hardly be called an arm — the fingers crunched, the bones separated, it was an entangled mass of flesh, like the roots of a tree unwilling to let go of each other. I thanked him for the description. He said he had shouted for help and rushed me into intensive care. What about the police, I asked. What about them, he replied. It was the right answer.

Over the next few days, or weeks — how can you tell time when you do not have a wrist for a watch? — I slept more than I was awake. I answered two questions over and over. Question: If I was the victim of a hit and run, why was I dropped off at the hospital? Answer: They must have sprouted a conscience after hitting me. Question: How did I know the orderly was telling the truth? Answer: There was no reason for him to lie.

I finally spoke to the doctor, the one who had done the cutting. He offered me his condolences and confirmed the orderly's story. He said I could see my arm if I wished to. The hospital did not keep the amputated limb itself, only a photograph of it. I would probably find it in a medical journal in the coming years, he said. I did not ask why. I told him I would very much like to see the photograph. He scooped it out of his pocket as if he were performing a magic trick for a dying child. Even in its mangled state, I recognized my arm. It had my burn mark.

The burn had been self-inflicted at age ten, one night when Mother was underneath the judge. Hungry, I had walked from my bedroom into the kitchen. I had put the stove on, for that was all I knew how to do, and let some water boil. I meant to burn them both — they were screaming and shouting so much anyway. As I watched the water boil, I thought of Father, and I understood why he never smiled, why he kept cutting himself with the razor blade even though he had finished shaving. I got Father's razor blade, dipped it in the boiling water and made a deep gash near the bicep of my left arm. Now Father and I shared the same sorrow. But unlike Father, I did not want to remind myself of Mother each day when I looked in the mirror. So I used my arm instead of my face. When Father came home, he dressed the wound. I told him I had no idea why I did it. He did not say much. Years later, the mark still remained in the shape of a crescent moon. I called it my burn mark because I was burning more than the water itself. But it was only in hospital that I realized its true worth. Without it, I would not have been able to identify my arm. Mother helped me without even knowing it.

Even with so much morphine in me, I was still able to think straight. Each day I floated above the hospital grounds, where everything was normal. An old man shot his wife in the temple, then collected the blood in a bedpan. A blind woman scooped her eyes out of their sockets with a spoon. She offered them to me but I told her I was on a strict liquid diet. So she mashed them for me. Besides me, these were the only two human patients in the hospital. The rest were all rabbits.

The day I was discharged, I looked into the other rooms on my way out. I kept seeing the rabbits. They were sad, as if they had lost their burrows. But I knew they would walk out whole and without shawls, unlike me. Why are these hospital corridors so long, I wondered. They never end. But I was happy. Unlike the sad rabbits, I was happy. The orderly stopped me just as I was about to step out.

He told me I could not take what I was carrying. He did not mean the shawl. Instead he looked down at what I held in my right hand. I told him that it was mine and I was taking it. Without it, what would I do? He said it wasn't mine. It belonged to the doctor and it wasn't even raining outside. I explained that rain had nothing to do with it. Then why was I carrying the doctor's umbrella, the orderly asked. He was mad. That was my arm I was carrying; it had been left hanging on a rack with a small note for me. I had to take it. But when the orderly took it from my hand, it *was* an umbrella. The small note was the manufacturer's label — export quality, "Made in Bhayandar."

The shawl kept slipping so I held it between my teeth and walked out on the street. If it slipped even once, everyone would be able to see my deformity. Then I would become a beggar, too. How would I hold my head high and look down upon them? I walked and walked and prided myself on having strong legs. If the arms were temporarily sick, at least the legs were still well. I would walk straight to my tree, a large tree with fat, deep roots. I would retrace my steps to find out what had happened. It was at the tree that I remembered having had two arms for the last time.

The tree was only a short distance from the hospital. That is the beauty of this city. Everything is close by. If you die, a cemetery is just around the corner. If you want to have someone killed, a contract killer is ready with a neatly typed contract. If you need a taxi, all you have to do is put your arm out and a taxi will run straight into it. I could go on and on. So I will. If you need to eat, ten hungry mouths are always open.

The tree was close to the egg man's stand, just below the Grant Road Bridge. I had eaten boiled eggs under it, drunk under it, made paid-for love under it, and from beneath its leaves I had looked at this city and wondered about its people. I had always laughed at their struggles. I had seen a man beating his wife on the bridge. He pulled her by the hair and she fell to the ground, and trains kept rumbling along below. I drank and wondered if the woman would ever strike back. She lay on the road with her head hung, unable to look at the man. She felt she deserved it. The man stood above her and waited for words to come out of her mouth so that he could shut them up forever.

When I went back to the tree after leaving the hospital, I saw everything in pairs. Stars clustered in twos, paper boats in the gutter-stream floated like couples. Even the trees were growing closer to each other, taunting me. My empty whiskey bottle was still there. I had drunk it full. Now it lay on a fat root and collected dust. What had I been doing here? I simply could not remember.

I decided that both the orderly and the doctor were lying about my arm. I started to dig the earth around the tree. My arm could have mistaken itself for a root and grown downward. I held my shawl between my teeth and dug with my hand. No, I thought, I must convince myself I am digging with my *hands*. I tore away at the soil and cursed it for luring my arm away. Stray dogs walked toward me, leaving their warm spots in the earth. They came slowly and stayed while I dug. I found eggshells, an empty packet of bread and a silver earring. There was blood all over it.

My fingers were bleeding and the skin had come off, so the pink of my flesh mixed with the red of blood and brown of earth. The dogs moved closer to me, and as I sat on the ground with the shawl between my teeth, they licked the blood off my fingers. Soon their hot tongues were satisfied. They sat by my feet as I looked up at the tree. It was then that I saw my arm.

It was in the tree. I pointed my arm out to the dogs but they were not surprised. I looked at the bridge to see if I could spot any night boys. I would pay them to climb the tree and lower my arm down. But then I saw another arm on the bridge. And another in a dog's mouth. Everyone had an arm, except me. I stared at the bark of the fat tree. A dog tugged at my shawl and tried to pull it down.

I let it.

PALACE TALKIE

I never went to the hospital again. Nor did I file a complaint with the police. I did not speak a word about my arm — not to myself even. I stayed silent for two whole months. I sold my apartment by the sea and moved into the sinking building. Since I did not speak, and communicated only in writing, the tenants assumed I was dumb. That way I did not have to answer anyone's questions. I convinced myself I had no idea how I had lost my arm.

And today, despite my efforts, I still do not know the story of my lost arm. After the giant pointed to my heart, I walked back up Love Lane, turned right, crossed the street, stepped on many dead vegetables, smelt them as well and went toward Palace Cinema for the 7 p.m. show. That is where I am now.

This cinema is a true palace. It looks very old. A group of old women is huddled outside — they must be the harem. One of them bends down to pick something up from the street. Perhaps she is trying to pick up the years that have fallen.

Thinking about the hospital has not been easy for me. In fact, the past two days have affected my brain. All these hints and clues, riddles and widdles, have confused me. I need to think less.

What better way to completely numb the brain than to watch that stupendous, magnificent, astounding, life-altering creation called The Hindi Movie?

Hindi movies are nothing more than our mothers shouting at us for not being good. They can also be used to sleep well. A lecture can be extremely soothing if you ignore it. I have not slept in two days. This hard seat with the crumbs of masala wafer on it will serve me well.

Life is full of melodrama. Talk from the heart, follow the light, respect the old and help others. We insist that we are tired of sermons, but let me tell you, that is an extra-large lie. There is enough sap in each of us to fill a thousand trees. We deserve all the melodrama we get. We are always greedy for more. Look at our movies. They are melodrama dipped in a tub full of honey, evil, stupidity, golden skin and happy endings. From goods to gods, we buy anything so long as the packing is earthy, preachy and full of dance.

The seats next to me are empty. The movie is not a hit. I did not read its name but it could very well be:

    a) Love Prevails

    b) Memories

    c) Lovers

There is a musty smell in the air. It could be due to:

    a) Socks being removed

    b) A dead rat

    c) A live rat

I see the heads of people. That is all you see in cinemas. Bald heads, oily heads, heads larger than domes or smaller than marbles, and heads that should be on beds because they are asleep. Lovers lean against each other, whispering into each other's ears, and little boys watch the screen, wanting to be like the hero. There is always one little boy who wants to be the heroine. I put my feet on the row of seats in front of me, but there is a loud hiss from behind. People will just not let me be.

I love the blackness, the loud filmi voices and the smell of sweat and old flowers. I do not know if it is with courage or with a lack of spine that I confess my love of Hindi movies. It is like loving a brother everybody hates. Even though you know your brother has faults, he is still your brother. When an outside person says bad things about him, you will kill that person. You are allowed to complain because he is yours. You can tell him that he is sad and good for nothing, but let anyone else say that and you will drink their khoon straight from the heart.

The movie has not started yet. First there is a mandatory announcement from the fire department: "In case of fire you will notice smoke. Do not panic. People seated on the left side of the theater please use the exit on the left. People on the right side of the theater please use the exit on the right." It is simple and full of common sense. I think there should also be an announcement from the director of the film: "This is a terrible movie. You know what will happen. Good will triumph over evil. The father-in-law will reform and accept the hero in the end. But what you do not know is that by mistake the heroine's nipple can be seen — twice."

I wish for a fire, tall and strong, to burn us all. The fire department does not want me to panic so I will watch the screen and let the monster flames eat me. I will not move until I have finished the movie, unless the fire finishes me first. I will be like the prophets of old, swallowed by fire and sent back to their homes far away from this earth and its Hindi movies.

I close my eyes and imagine my place in history. I will be the world's first crippled prophet. Even though I will heal and cure everyone else, I will remain without an arm. If my disciples ask me why, the answer will be because I wish to suffer. If I end my suffering, I will lose the power to heal. I have no teachings to offer, I will say. All I have is this terrible absence, this long draft of air that makes even God go cold.

When I think of it, I *have* suffered as a prophet would. Aren't all prophets beaten as children for being different? If the prophets of old believed in God too much, I did not believe in him at all. I was lashed for it by my school principal.

Mr. Old's cane is very long and thick. I have seen horses in hill stations being whipped with these canes. I can tell from the way it cuts air that even the air hurts. These canes are meant for animals. I stand in Mr. Old's office with my hands behind my back and my back very straight. Our school principal does not like boys who slouch.

"That boy is a good student," he says. "I am told he is a *very* good student."

"Yes, Sir," I say.

"I am told he got the highest mark in English."

The entire school is obsessed with English. They must all go back to Britain then. Play cricket with the Englishmen, fetch their balls when they reach the beautiful white fence, and serve tea to them on the lawn.

"So you agree that he is good."

"Yes, Sir."

"Then what in God's name were you thinking when you brought that desk down on him?"

I do not answer. I want to ask questions of my own. What *is* God's name? Is he Indian or British? Does he play kabbaddi like Indians do, or is he a football hooligan?

"There *is* no God," I say.

"What?"

He does not even ask me to lean on the table. He strikes hard and I can see the hate in his face. I am sure there is no God now. If Mr. Old believes in him, God will stop existing out of sheer shame. There will be at least twenty hits. Mr. Old has a terrible magic cane. I see all his certificates on the wall. I find them very hard to read. Not because I am stupid, but because of the pain.

The second blow hurts more than the first. The third one hurts the most. Just like words. People say that when hurtful words are repeated often enough they lose their sting. That is false. You never get used to bad things.

There is a fourth hit. And a fifth. He does not aim, just strikes like a blind man. They land on my face, arm, back and chest. I do not cry. I try to read a certificate, any certificate, but they are all going blurry. The caning goes on and on and I lose count. I scream out loud a few times, but like a man. By the time Mr. Old is satisfied, I can barely stand. I cannot even hear too well. He says something about me being expelled from school and what a poor job my mother has done. He has convinced Viren's mother to file a criminal complaint so that I learn a lesson. Let it bring shame upon this school. His duty is to reform me. Mr. Old says that Viren will be great when he grows up and if he does lose an eye then I have done the devil's work and I hope I am happy.

But I am not happy. I am very upset. I did not mean to blind Viren. It was a mistake. I do not feel bad because of Viren. I feel bad because I was not careful.

※

I wake up to the light of the movie screen and realize that Mr. Old is old news. I must have slept through the intermission. Luckily the movies are all the same.

It is a crucial climax scene. The hero is in danger. The villain has cornered him near an old temple. They are both tired from running. The background music is just as tiring. The villain leans against a large tree and twirls his handlebar moustache. He points a gun at the hero.

"If you have drunk your mother's milk, throw your gun down," says the hero.

"I have drunk every type of milk," says the villain. "Mother's milk, cow's milk and milk that is like silk. But I'm going to kill you with this gun only."

"In your case, there's no difference between mother's milk and cow's milk," says the hero. He looks shocked by his own intelligence.

"What?"

"Your mother is a cow."

An insult to one's mother is worse than being called an untouchable. The loss of a country can be tolerated, but not the loss of ma ka doodh. The villain throws the weapon to the ground. It lands in a puddle of brown water.

A fight ensues. It is dramatic and goes on for very long. So does the music.

Just when the villain is choking the hero against the steps of the temple, the heroine appears. She is a mixture of a doll and a prostitute. It is hard to imagine that one day she will also be a mother and someone will fight for her dignity.

She grabs the gun in the brown puddle. She points it at the villain. The fighting stops. The music does not.

"Twenty years ago you killed my mother," she tells the villain. "Now it's your turn to die."

Even though he is not meant to, the hero interjects, "But twenty years ago *my* mother was killed, too. Does that mean we had the same mother?" A tear wells in his right eye. "We are brother–sister," he says. "We cannot sing and run around trees and make passionful romance."

"Shut up, you farmer," blares the heroine. "I should kill you both. Him for murder, you for stupidity."

"What will you do after I'm dead?" asks the hero.

He runs his hands through his wet black hair and puts on his doleful look.

"I will bury you," she replies.

"That's not what I meant," he clarifies.

"Quiet. Who's holding the gun?"

Then the villain speaks, to buy time until that point in the plot where he strangles the heroine by the neck, and presses her close to his body.

"Don't you cremate the body?" interferes the villain.

"I will bury you. I will chop off all your parts and bury them," says the heroine.

There is a close-up of the heroine. She is looking directly at me: "Bury. Understand? It's what you do when death comes. Bury."

Two gunshots are fired but I do not see the screen. Instead I think of Abdul's words: *Get rid of the finger, it reeks of death.* May the crow strike me down if I am lying. I must relinquish the finger. Decayed, it was no longer of any use to the leper. Just as he passed it on to me, I must do the same. Only then will I come closer to an arm. I know I must bury the finger because it is dead. But I must put it in a coffin first. I must go back to Mr. P.

MR. P AND THE DARK TORPEDO

Even though it is night, Mr. P's coffin enterprise is open. This makes sense to me. People die at all times. At night, all of us leave our bodies and visit our loved ones in the spirit world. A few of us do not come back. We look at our body from up above and wonder why we would want to repossess it. That is how we die in our sleep.

When I step into his office, Mr. P puts the phone down. He shouts toward the back of his coffin enterprise and asks not to be disturbed. There is no answer. Seven large coffins are neatly stacked on an iron stand. They are brown and made of the finest wood. The lowest one is labelled *Made in England*. First the British kill us. Then we import their coffins. How touching.

"Mr. P," I say. "I have come with the finger."

He does not seem perplexed, nor does he give any indication that he knows what I am talking about.

"I want to preserve the finger. It was given to me as a mark of respect," I add. "It is dead now, so I must bury it."

Mr. P points to a photograph album on the table before him. The word LOVE is written in gold letters on the cover. I assume I am meant to glance through the album.

"Don't worry," he says. "They're not wedding pictures. A man in your state can get quite depressed thinking about weddings."

"Very."

When I open the album I see pictures of coffins: finger coffins, arm coffins, toe coffins. It surprises me how much I do not know about this city. Tomorrow I might meet a midget who is ten feet tall, a butcher who sells newborn babies, a boxer who works as an anesthetist in a hospital by knocking patients senseless. In this city, birds are forced to crawl and rats can fly if they use their tails correctly. When I think about this city, it is almost as if it does not exist. It is a body floating on air, and landing whenever it gets tired. That is why it is so noisy. The din is the sound of it panting.

While I gaze through the album, Mr. P reads a newspaper. His spectacles are perched on a fat nose. I select a dark coffin with a metallic glaze. It will serve as a contrast to the dull hue the finger has acquired. I point to the picture and look at Mr. P.

"Why do you call yourself Mr. P?" I ask.

"There are almost fourteen thousand eunuchs in the city," he says, ignoring me. He takes his spectacles off and looks at me. He taps the newspaper with his knuckles. I do not know what this interesting statistic has to do with the question I have just asked. I stare at him blankly.

"Out of those fourteen thousand, only half are original eunuchs." He raises an eyebrow.

"That's sad," I say.

"No, it's good! It means only seven thousand are castrated. The others were born useless, so no harm done."

Mr. P turns toward the back of the shop and shouts: "Quiet in there! I'm talking here."

I do not hear anything. I wonder if this is a test. So I shout, too. "Yes, please! Keep the volume to a minimum!"

On the wall I see family pictures neatly framed. One in particular stands out. It is in black and white, and it shows a stout man, a dark woman, two beautiful children and an old lady. The old lady's face is circled in red felt pen. Strangely, all the photographs on the wall have one or two persons who are marked in red.

"You're wondering about the red circles," Mr. P remarks.

"Yes."

"They are the dead ones."

"Ah."

"I made coffins for them all."

"Wonderful."

"Thank you."

"You're welcome."

"You want to know a secret?"

"I love secrets."

"I circled one by mistake."

"What do you mean?"

"That old woman in the far corner."

"Yes?" He refers to the photograph I saw first.

"She was my wife's friend. I found that family photograph at home and circled her by mistake and put it up in my shop, thinking I had made a coffin for her. She had given the photo to my wife to show off her grandchildren."

"I don't like show-offs."

"She died the very day I circled her."

"How sad."

"No. How coincidental."

"Extremely."

"Stand very still."

"What?"

"Don't move."

Mr. P ducks his head below the counter and snaps back like a puppet. He holds a small camera in his hands. He shoots me. I feel like a soldier who has just been tricked by the enemy.

"Why did you do that?"

"I'm going to circle you, too."

"I'm going to die?"

"I hope so. It's my hobby. To take pictures of strangers and then mark them for death. I want to see if it's a gift I have or if it was just a one-time random happening with that old woman."

"I wish you well," I say.

"How kind."

We do not speak for a while. I think of my photograph developing. I hope he took only the face. But what if both arms show up in the picture? That would be nice. I would *prance* if that happened. I have never pranced, or even thought of prancing before.

"You've chosen the Dark Torpedo," Mr. P says.

"Dark Torpedo?"

"That's the name of the coffin."

"When will it be ready?"

He gets up and unlocks a small cabinet that is placed near a wooden stool. The shelves of the cabinet are lined with red felt. He removes what I assume is the coffin. It is wrapped in white cloth. He takes off the cloth and caresses the Dark Torpedo. It looks better in reality than it does in the photograph. He pushes it toward me. I open the lid and see the indent of a finger: streamlined for the tip, gradually fattening at the center, and receding toward the base. Just like the leper's.

"Go ahead. Try it out," he coaxes.

I place the finger in the coffin. I feel sad, as though I am parting with a dear friend. Without it, my journey ends. Maybe I should buy my own coffin. I do not tell Mr. P that I ordered one over the phone only a day ago. He did not like me over the phone. I am much more charming in person.

"Learn to let go," says Mr. P. "Only then will you receive."

He adjusts his spectacles and looks outside at the street. There is a church opposite, with a signboard that promises to save alcoholics. Three trees stand near the church steps. Sometimes drunks climb the trees instead of the church steps. But God does not mind. Only the priests do.

I snap the coffin lid shut. "Do I leave the finger with you?" I ask.

"What for?"

"So you can direct me further."

"That will be two thousand rupees."

"Two thousand! But it's such a small coffin."

"Do you know anyone else who makes one?"

"No."

"Am I wrong in assuming that you can afford it?"

"I . . ."

"Then two thousand rupees cash. Take the coffin with you." He raises his voice. "And for the last time, quiet back there!"

GURA AND THE EGG-MAN

I know what Mr. P means by sending me away with the coffin. He means the same thing that Gura did, the floating beggar who directed me to the In-charge. I must get used to this absence. My palm is too full of the past to be able to receive anything.

Perhaps I need to talk with Gura again. I have not seen him since our first meeting yesterday morning. Floating beggars have no home, but at the end of the day they all eat together. They collect at the egg-man's, opposite A-1 Restaurant, under the Grant Road Bridge. Then they float away into the night again.

When I think about it, the egg-man looks a lot like Gura. It could be because I have seen the egg-man only at night. If there is even a slight similarity between people, they look more alike at night.

It is not because of the darkness. It has to do with the moon.

My old servant told me this, and I have expanded and expounded her theory. The moon, she used to say, was an evil fishmonger before it was the moon. That is why the moon is so far away from us. It stinks. Now, being the moon, and out of fish, it plays tricks on earth people. One of its favorite games is to make people look alike. It reflects only those parts of a person's face that look similar to the parts on another person's face. My servant was beautiful (so she thought) and her sister was ugly (true, true). When the moon was out, people would tell the two sisters that they looked alike. During the day, they did not. So it is quite a solid theory. Moonlight can make two mooncalves think they are moonlighting as replicas of each other. It is a moonstruck theory, which can be easily shaken and disproved by a moonquake.

As I approach the egg-man, I yearn not for his bhurji-pao but for a window. There should be windows available to all unhappy people. Let us say you are walking on the road and you have the sudden urge to die. (Some people crave death as they do cigarettes.) If the craving gets too intense, a window should appear. You can jump through the window and plunge to your death. Suicide takes too much planning. It then ceases to be suicide and becomes murder of the self. If a window opened out of nowhere, my death would be accidental. The last person to understand this would be the egg-man.

There are two girls at the egg-man's stand. I recognize them as dancers from Topaz. I do not want to see them because they remind me of *her*. In every man's life, there will be *that one woman*. He knows he should treat her well; he knows he should open her hair gently and let her rivers of black touch the floor. But because she is stronger than he is, he will separate her thighs again and again so that when she is least expecting it, he can tell her he is leaving her.

That one woman will look into your eyes while holding you. She will touch you, make you feverish, and ask you if that is really your thickness she is holding or a bijli ka khamba. When you tell her that it is no bolt of lightning, she will tell you that you are wrong. She will fly you to heaven. After you have flown and exchanged your heart for a larger one, she will make you sleep in her lap and she will play with your hair. Only then will you believe in God and ask for no further proof of his creation. But again, even to know God, you need money.

As I look at the bar dancers, who eat their eggs so beautifully, I am taken to the edge of her bed, where I stood and undressed while she looked outside. The streetlights shone on the movie posters.

That night, Malaika was not happy. I had drunk too much.

Malaika. That very name makes me want her to bear my children. Seventy times. It is the best name in the world. God should be called Malaika. Then everybody will love him.

That night Malaika was not happy.

"Your drinking makes you less of a man," she said.

"Come here," I told her.

But she sat by her dressing table and looked at the moon. The flowers in her hair were white, or orange, or an evil green.

"Not tonight," she said. "This night is bad."

"I will make it badder."

"You love me?"

I talked to her face in the mirror. It was less beautiful but easier to remember. "Tonight I do," I said.

"What about tomorrow?"

"If I can still afford to love you, I will."

"Means?"

"You're expensive."

"I'm worried about you."

"Then come and suck my worries away."

The window next to the dresser opened with the wind. A car horn entered the room. Buffalo horn, Fiat, 1970s.

"I keep thinking something is going to happen to you," she said.

"You're right."

"Even you feel it?"

"Something happens to me every time you kiss me. Will you marry me?"

"No."

"Not even for a day?"

"Just for one day?"

"I will love you more in one day than other men can in a lifetime."

"You talk like a bad poet."

"What's a poet?"

"Someone who means one thing and says another."

Once more the car horn entered the room. Smoke from a cooking fire as well. The flowers in her hair were green. They did things behind her head that she could not see. I did not like those flowers.

"Come here," I said.

"You don't have to pay me tonight."

"Why not?"

"Tonight, I will pay *you.*"

"I'd love that."

"But you won't fetch much."

"Then I'll work extra hard."

The sari she wore was almost transparent, and her nipples rose through her blouse as if they wished to speak. *Her skin is so smooth*

I could slip on it if I walked, I thought. *I love this woman.*

I held her face in both my hands. I wanted to call out her name. I wanted to call her by a hundred names. I wanted to call her name a hundred times. I told her.

"You're so silly. Like a child."

"Malaika," I said.

"What."

"Start counting."

I moved close to her lips until their redness could kill me.

"Malaika," I said.

"Yes."

"That was one," I said. "Malaika."

"Two," she played along.

"Malaika."

"Three."

"Malaika."

On some days you can count like a gambler and still lose. Even after one hundred I could not stop. Instead of getting less drunk, I flew across the room — over her dresser, along the cracks in the stone and under the wobbling fan. The flowers in her hair were so green that each time I tried to break them loose, the color rubbed off on my hands. It seemed as if both my hands had been dipped in a mossy, slimy pool of water. The next second I had no hands. They had been cut off at the wrists. Then the elbows were gone. I wanted to ask Malaika how she knew the night was bad, but all she would say was, "You don't have to pay me."

The two bar dancers have finished eating their meal and sway toward their cars. They are rich, earning as much as chartered accountants do, and their cars are more expensive. Dancers can be accountants if they want to. It might take work, but it can be done. But why count numbers when you can dance to them?

"How are you?" asks the egg-man. His cart has been painted yellow since I last saw him. Without waiting for me to respond, he says, "You're hungry. You need eggs."

"I need a window to die," I say.

"No stylish talk here. Say straight." He grinds his teeth and lets out a grunt.

"One bhurji-pao," I order.

"Should I throw lots of masala?"

"No, it's hard on my stomach."

"Less spicy then. Sit."

"Where?"

"Lean on the bonnet."

He indicates a white Maruti with his head as he breaks the eggs into two and lets them fry on an oily iron plate. I can see my large, fat tree in the distance. The stray dogs still hover around it. They are so sick that they look like ghosts of dogs.

"Why do you not want masala? It does not taste the same if it's not spicy."

"My stomach," I remind him.

"Why worry about your stomach when you don't have an arm?"

"You're right," I say. "Throw lots of masala."

He slaps a thick red paste onto the plate. I wonder if the ghost dogs can smell it.

"I will make you burn in delight like a woman of the night," he says. "You'll go home and still be on fire. You'll need a fire engine to calm you down. No, even if they put the hose in your mouth you'll still not get relief. But for a few hours you'll forget that you don't have an arm because the burning will be so good."

The sari shops are all closed for the night. Beside them is a makeshift temple with oil lamps in its hutch. They are still burning because there is no wind. Five children sleep near the shutters of the sari shop. They snore in peace; they do not hate the world. Only those who have beds hate the world. The god in the makeshift temple knows this. That is why he lets poverty grow; he does not want his children to own beds and hate the world.

The egg-man sprinkles salt, slaps an orange mixture into the existing egg paste. A prod here, a poke there, a few droplets of his sweat dip in, sizzle-sizzle.

"Is that your money box?" he asks, pointing to the finger coffin.

I do not feel like explaining. So I put the Dark Torpedo in my pocket and pull out a ten-rupee note.

"Is this enough?" I ask.

"I made this with love. Now it's up to you to pay with love."

"More than ten rupees?"

"Your love is weak. My love is real and strong."

"Fifteen rupees okay?"

"Right now you love me like a brother or sister. I made bhurji for you like a naughty, spicy lover."

"Is twenty rupees fine?"

"Yes. You are my true love. Romeo–Juliet, Laila–Majnu no class. It should be put in all the scriptures and literatures that the realest love came from a cripple to an egg-man and exactly opposite versa."

"It's sad that no one knows how much you love me."

He puts his hand on his heart. "If that is how you feel, then feel no more." He shouts, "Help!"

I look around but there is no one. I recall that Mr. P talked to imaginary people as well. Perhaps it is a new practice in the city. But why invent people when millions already exist?

"Someone help! Come here and see our love."

I repeat what I did at Mr. P's. I imitate the egg-man: "Come here and watch two lovers."

"Who are you talking to?"

"The same person you are talking to."

Just then I hear a scraping sound. It comes from underneath the egg-cart. There is a loud bump and the cart rattles a bit. The egg-man reacts quickly and ensures that none of the plates or food land on the street.

"Gura, is that you?" asks the egg-man.

"It is."

"What are you doing underground?"

"Sleeping."

Did Gura know I was looking for him? Was he hiding from me? There is still no sign of his face. I hope he does not intend on conversing from below the cart.

"Did you get drunk again?" asks the egg-man.

"Yes," says Gura.

"Come out of there. I don't want people to think negative things."

"Like what?"

"Like what you could be doing to me from under there," says the egg-man with a sheepish grin.

Gura scuttles out from below the egg-cart. He is not surprised to see me at all. Maybe that is why he does not acknowledge me.

"We want you to see our love," says the egg-man.

"Brotherly," I say. "All brotherly."

"You think I'm a fool? There is no such thing as brotherly love!" says Gura.

"Gura, calm down," says the egg-man.

"Right in front of my eyes you're doing this!"

"Gura, we were doing nothing," I say.

Then Gura starts mumbling. He eats up his words, swallows them like a goblin chomping up tiny living letters at random. The remaining letters flee for their lives, and even though they try to collect themselves, they make no sense at all.

In a fit, Gura lifts the egg-man's iron frying pan and flings it onto the bonnet of the white Maruti. Even the egg-man is startled. Next to go are the small plastic containers that hold masalas. Gura opens them and sprinkles the powder into my eyes. My eyes sting and water. Through the haze, trees fall, rivers dry up and a midget rides a tricycle. I can see only that which is not before me. Mad women, blue dogs, orange robes and deep wells. I hear children screaming, swords clashing, prayers failing.

Then everything goes quiet.

I look for the egg-man and Gura but they are nowhere.

It is too dark to see, but I sense a light, a slight varnish, around an object a man holds in his hands. He strokes it methodically, as if he is giving it a new coat of light with his fingers.

"Mr. P makes good coffins," he says in a resounding voice. He speaks with the speed and grace of a carrier pigeon in flight. The glaze around the Dark Torpedo is a sheet of dark ice.

"You were ready to let go, so I helped myself," he says.

I can trace the finger through the coffin. I try to see the man's face but only his long, matted hair is visible.

"Who are you?" I ask him.

"Baba Rakhu," he replies.

PET DUNGEON

In the dim light, human limbs slowly appear on the wall. I see all kinds: dark ones, long ones, stunted ones. They are neatly packed in plastic sheets as they hang shamelessly, suits and shirts waiting to be picked.

"Welcome to my khopcha," says Baba Rakhu. "My pet dungeon that will save the world. How many men are without arms? How many women are without legs? It is shameful when the eunuch-dogs of this city roam freely."

The organization of the arms and legs is meticulous — they are labelled with names in alphabetical order; they shine a little, coated with a substance to preserve them.

Baba Rakhu clasps his matted hair above his head with both hands. "What are you thinking, brother? There is no shame in buying arms. It is like buying anything else."

A hairy arm dangles above me like the leather support strap in a bus. I want to take the black shawl that Baba has draped over his shoulders and cover the arm with it.

"You are what . . . five feet seven? Short one you are. So you will need short arm."

What I need is to beat my conscience to a thin paste. I try not to imagine how Baba must acquire these limbs. He selects a short, pale arm, slightly hairy, with a white scar on the wrist. He strokes it lovingly as if he is a vendor displaying quality silk. Without removing its plastic wrapping, he holds it in place of my missing arm. I quiver as the arm touches my skin. Even my stump is repulsed by something that should seem familiar. I move away.

"What are you doing?" he shouts. "Stay still. Trial fitting."

"So you do sell arms and legs . . ."

"You act as though I am selling guns."

"There must be at least . . ." I try counting the limbs in front of me.

He uses the arm in his hand as a pointer and instructs, "Twenty right legs, twenty left legs, both male and female. Seven pairs of arms. And seven single ones for gentlemen like you."

I imagine my body if I buy an arm. I will stand naked in front of the mirror and dance, count my fingers repeatedly as though I am the first to discover that humans have ten fingers. I will use my new arm to scratch an itch on my neck, to turn the pages of a newspaper. I might even learn sign language and never speak again.

"So, brother, only twenty thousand rupees for this arm, including surgery." He looks at me with eyes of charcoal, his long beard a tangle of snakes that will come to life any minute and bite me for being greedy.

He places the arm once more against my stump. He shakes his head. "This one does not suit you. Not to worry. I will get one to match your size and skin tone. It will only take a day or two."

He places the arm back on its rack. "Twenty thousand rupees. Cash only. And I don't give receipt."

"The price is fine with me," I reply. I am sure this is my lost arm talking. Or the unbought arm — maybe it is lonely. "I'm worried about something else."

"The surgery? That is only a term I use. There will be no knives and blood, or any bogus rituals. Once I get an arm, I simply attach it to your body. It is a gift I have. If you believe in God, call it God-given."

"The surgery is not a concern," I answer.

"Then what, brother? If money and health do not bother you, what lunatic flesh are you made of?"

"Where do you get these arms?"

"Do you check where the vegetable vendor gets his stock? Do you know every detail about the fish that are sold at your doorstep?"

"This is different."

"Only if you let it be."

"But I need to know if . . ."

"Need to know what? I offer you a commodity that is unattainable and what do I get in return? I will forgive your insolence only because you have proved your worth by preserving the finger. Otherwise, step outside. The scenery will be breathtaking there, once I put your face in the gutter."

At any moment, his beard will spurt poison in my face, blind me for not seeing in the first place. As he shouts, the arms on the wall move — a twitch, a flick of their wrists, fingers rise to point at me. In the corner opposite us there is a pair of female legs. They tremble as though their flesh has been beaten, smacked as sorely as a disobedient child's. Baba breathes into my face. With each exhalation, a germ of fear is born within me.

"You young people complain too much," he says. "You lose an arm, you complain. Someone offers you one, you complain. If you have the money, buy it. Think of it as an orange. It might grow in someone else's garden, but if you are hungry you will eat it."

"An orange."

"An organ transplant, then. No incompetent doctor will meddle with the fitting. It is Baba Rakhu's guarantee, brother. To date, I have fixed two hundred cripples."

"In the case of a transplant there is a donor. I doubt these arms are donated."

"A minor technicality," he continues. "I want to help you. You seem like a good person, although . . . your skin is a little pale. I will do what I have not done for any customer before. You will learn how I obtain my stock."

He is convinced that he is selling oranges.

"If you choose not to use my services after that, so be it. If you go to the police, there's a special place reserved for your other arm right there in the corner."

If I retreat now, I am dead anyway. I have met Baba Rakhu and seen his pet dungeon. Are some of these limbs customers' limbs? It is so dark here. Hell must be like this. Only less organized.

I ask, "Who do you take from? Do you target the poor and hard-working as well, or is it only the eunuch-dogs you despise?"

"Before you behave like a third-class journalist, did you understand the condition I just set you?"

"Yes," I tell him. "If I'm convinced, I buy an arm. If I'm not convinced, I walk away. If I run to the police, I lose the other."

"It is settled, then. You shall witness the buying. Before we go arm shopping, we must eat. Please serve yourself," he says.

But there is not a morsel of rice around, or, for that matter, a morsel of anything I recognize as human morality.

Baba motions to the arms and legs. "All you can eat, brother. America style."

Legs swim before my eyes and I picture chili powder being sprinkled on them for flavor. Because Baba Rakhu speaks of America I see salt and pepper shakers. I imagine the legs being chopped into edible pieces and placed on banana leaves, because that is an Indian custom. Nausea overtakes me and the snakes in Baba's beard bicker amongst themselves over who gets me first. I throw up — it is the only act that seems dignified in this depraved brothel.

I hear Baba's voice and the snakes are gone. "Brother, you are a weakling. It is unwise to be so delicate in the present day."

"Perhaps we could talk a little more."

"Talk is for politicians. We simple folk must simply exchange arms."

"But I was hoping . . ."

"Hope is the poor man's burden. Why are you carrying it?"

Mockery. We all hate being subjected to it, and yet it is our favorite subject.

"Do you have a shopping bag?" he asks me.

"What for?"

"To put the arm in."

I see the flying cockroaches again. I am confused because there are both brown and black ones. They act as if they are friends. Good and evil holding hands, dancing like children. They are celebrating that I have come to this place. They sing a song, the type bandits sing on horses, and it is lovely. Then they stop flying. They lie flat on their backs, wings spread out, looking at the ceiling. In a minute, they are dead.

ABDUCTION

A lightbulb looms over Baba's head. It gives his silver matted hair a luminescence fit only for the wise and the holy. After an hour of window shopping, we are back in his pet dungeon.

"This is terrible," I say. "I don't even know this man."

I look at the man in the khaki uniform, tied to a chair. Unshaven and dirty, he is in a room with limbs for curtains. Baba positions the man under the lightbulb.

"I don't even know this man," I repeat.

"Then next time we should abduct someone you know."

With his black shawl still draped over him, Baba is wearing the sheen of crows. He puts his face very close to the man's. The man's neck is limp. He is a drunken person who has passed out in front of a TV. His face is blank.

"For your moral satisfaction, I will demonstrate why this man here is a candidate. I will show you the criteria for his selection," says Baba.

I want to tell Baba that he is depraved, that he is no visionary but a fraudulent mound of flesh. My thoughts bombard the pores of his skin but cannot penetrate.

"There are many reasons that make him an ideal choice," he says. Baba taps the man's temple with his knuckles. "They are all neatly tucked away in here. Any suggestions on how to retrieve them?"

I am not enjoying this. I have just helped Baba transport a man in the trunk of an old Ambassador in a manner suited to a sack of old potatoes. We held him by his arms and legs as we carried him to Baba's limb emporium. I had not noticed the low door at the end of this room. Who would notice a door when limbs hang merrily above your head? A carpet of dust lies on the floor.

Baba taunts me further: "It is simple for me to attach an arm. But to bring a man back to consciousness, I have not mastered that yet."

"Throw water on his face."

"You have the brain of a toilet! The body is scientific. It is not a radio — bang it once and it will work again." He looks at me with a raised eyebrow. "But let us do what you say. Otherwise you will complain."

Baba walks to the low door at the far end. I hear the clack of utensils. Baba returns with a steel glass in one hand.

"We have here the product of your toilet mind," he says. "Throw water on his face."

He extends the steel glass my way. I do not take it. He throws the contents of the glass on my face.

"Your skin needs it," he smirks. "It is so pale. Come under this bulb. Let me examine it."

I look around at the skin on the arms and legs that hang from the walls. My flesh resembles that of the preserved — shades of scaly pinks, browns and blacks that are acquired only in dark places. I wipe the water off my face. The little that is left on my lips, I lick.

"Time to awaken our sleeping booty!" he sings.

He presses the back of the man's neck with both his thumbs. He twists the neck sideways, first gently, then with a quick jerk. I think of my barber.

The man squints, the light further polishing the glaze of his oily black hair. Baba pokes his head into the man's line of sight like a hand puppet.

"Baba Rakhu!" shouts the man.

"See how famous I am. Everybody knows my name. I like my name. Don't you think it is nice?" he asks me as he circles the man.

The man has realized that he is bound to a chair. His gaze does not leave Baba.

"Baba Rakhu!" he says again.

Baba slaps him. It is a very calm slap — forceful, yet calm. "Quiet. Don't overdo it. Overdoing things is the number one problem in our country. In our movies also. We don't need people over-killing in real life."

Baba walks toward one wall, where only arms are displayed. He runs across the width and plucks at them — they are the strings of his sitar. "Be subtle, like me," he tells the man.

It is obvious that the man does not like Baba's orchestration. "No! Not that! I'm innocent."

"What a positive attitude he has. Guilty as a beast of burden but denies it," he tells me. "Why can't you be more like him?"

I do not know what to say. Perhaps it is because I am guilty, too. At least a bank robber uses his arms to steal money. I am using money to steal an arm.

"Why are you helping me?" I ask.

Baba breaks into laughter. This scares the man on the chair, who struggles to break loose.

"I'm not *helping* you. I'm selling you an arm for money. Rich cripples like you fund my enterprise so I can afford to give limbs to the poor."

"So it's only about the money, then."

"What else?"

"Then why didn't you contact me directly? Why did Gura and the In-charge lead me here?"

"They are part of the fine print," he smirks. "You need to earn your arm back. Even though you are paying for it. Now stop being tragic and concentrate on this specimen who is about to lose his arm."

Baba looks at the man on the chair again. Sweat sticks to his body like fear.

"You've made a mistake," he tells Baba. "You've got the wrong person. I have done nothing."

"You lie like the eunuch-dog you are about to become. But since I am fair, I will give you a choice. Would you rather lose an arm or leg?"

Then he points to me and whispers in the man's ear: "Perhaps I will leave that decision to this delicate object here. He is very much a part of this."

"I am not," I say.

"Enough of this time-wasting argument. After I am done with him, you will have to decide whether you wish to buy an arm or not."

I feel small discussing this in front of a man whose arm is in question. I feel small but calm, because I still do not think it possible.

"Do you beat your wife?" Baba asks the man.

"I'm innocent, I swear," says the man.

"I wish to teach you something," Baba tells me. "It will be useful when you get married to find out if your wife is playing someone else's flute."

He rips open the man's khaki shirt. Buttons fall to the floor. "No guns or pitiful devices of torture to make you talk," he reassures the man.

He fidgets with the man's nipples as though he is operating an old TV knob. I do not know if the man is as unsure of Baba's actions as I am. The nipples are brown and small. They point well, though.

"The nipples are the organs that control the honesty and dishonesty glands of the human body," Baba instructs us. "We must find the right channel by twisting them." He asks the man, "Do you beat your wife?"

"No!"

"This man's reception is bad."

He tweaks the nipples again. The man yelps a little.

"Tell me."

"It's not true," says the man.

Now he turns the right nipple clockwise, very slowly.

"Answer me," Baba says.

"Let me go!"

"We are still on the wrong channel."

He turns both nipples clockwise.

"Do you beat your wife?"

"I . . . I'm not sure," says the man.

"You already know this man," I say. "This is a joke."

"Quiet. We're getting closer," says Baba.

He turns the nipples clockwise once more and keeps them twisted at that angle. The man giggles. His eyes are watery; the thin film makes them look silly and dazed.

"We are definitely moving in the right direction," concludes Baba.

I do not move. I simply watch this charade.

"For the last time, do you hit your wife?"

"She deserves it!"

Baba releases the nipples. "Feel free to garland me anytime," he tells me.

"Do you expect me to believe in this?" I ask.

"Let me assure you that by the end of this little talk, you will. Now you question him. He will answer. Right now, he is in another room."

"You mean another plane of existence?"

"Nothing that fancy. If we are in the basement, he is in the attic. He feels safe there, eats sweets and plays with toys. He does not know what dishonesty is while he is there."

"Cockfights," says the man.

"Is he talking to us?" I ask.

"To everyone and no one. He's talking to himself. His body secretes only honesty from its glands right now."

"I had a cock," says the man. "Killer was his name. He was a terrific fighter. Grown men wept when they saw Killer fight. He was as elegant as a bird. He *was* a bird — but what I mean is, he had style. I bet heavily on him and he made me lots of money."

The man looks directly at four pairs of legs to his left and recites this. I wonder if he see cocks fighting in their place.

"When Killer was not fighting, I let the little girls and boys of our gully play with him. 'Uncle, can we play with your cock?' they used to ask me. Because of the children's petting, Killer got weak. In a crucial match against a cock from South India, Killer was killed. That day, I went home and beat my wife."

"So he hit his wife once. It's wrong, but does he need to lose an arm?" I ask.

"Was that the only time you hit her?" Baba asks the man.

"Of course not. The day after we got married I slapped her because she refused to press my feet. Can you imagine? After I opened her petals so delicately on our wedding night."

"Isn't he worthy?" asks Baba.

The man continues: "The next time was two days later. She went to her mother's house without telling me. What if I got hungry or needed water? Then a week later, she spoke to our neighbor. He is male! Beatings became regular after that. Because I hit her so much, her skin stayed blue and hard as stone. That made her unattractive. So I had to seek pleasure elsewhere. It was an inconvenience, so I hit her again. Then her lips would swell up. She would look worse. What a cycle."

I hope he runs out of toys or sweets, gets bored and climbs down from the attic to this dungeon. The casualness of his revelations is turning him into a casualty.

"Stop," I say.

"You're the one who needed justification," Baba reminds me. "Now hear him out."

"No, make him stop."

"One last question," Baba asks the man. "If India and Pakistan played a cricket match, who would you support?"

The man looks to the ceiling and nods his head a couple of times. "Pakistan. Our team is unpredictable. Indian batsmen cannot face fast bowling. They jump and duck at the same time."

"I must kill this unpatriotic coconut," says Baba.

"Because he does not like the Indian cricket team?" I ask.

"Absolutely. Now all that's left is the cutting."

Baba happily performs a sawing action. He does not mean the kind of cutting I used to have in school with my buttered bread.

I would do anything for a hot and steamy cutting from Lucky Moon right now. I could sip calming tea and watch.

"Help me return him to the car trunk," says Baba.

"Again?"

"Yes, we must amputate in his natural habitat."

I miss the flying cockroaches. Their death has emptied me.

***

As the car moves, the city's homeless appear and disappear in fast blurs. Young boys smoke ganja in dim light. Men blindfolded by a dark sky sleep on the footpath in neat rows. These are men who walk the earth, build houses in the shade and smuggle in traces of warm light when life is not looking.

I hear the murmur of mosquitoes. They tell me I have used my hands wrongly. I passed by the houses of these men and looked through their windows. Instead of helping, I used my hands to blindfold myself. I read my own palm and overlooked the torn elephants that lay by my side.

There is a red icebox between Baba and me on the front seat. It looks beautiful and wet in this heat, with water trickling down its sides. The chair-man is in the backseat clapping his hands and bobbing his head from side to side. He is still in the attic of his own candor, enjoying his collection of broken dolls.

Soon we approach a line of parked taxis. I have never been in this part of the city before. There are no taxiwalas around. I do not understand why this is so; they always sleep on the bonnets of their cars with their shirts open and chest hair flying in the breeze. All the taxi meters are down for the night. The taxiwalas are probably lined up to buy petrol for the next morning. Baba stops the car.

The air is flat and even the dust seems exhausted, unable to rise and cause discomfort.

"Lead us to your taxi," he tells the chair-man.

So the chair-man is a taxiwala. He points to the third taxi from the front.

"Bring the icebox with you," Baba tells me as he steps out of the car.

"Please sit on the bonnet," Baba tells the chair-man.

I place the icebox on the ground. The chair-man quickly plops onto the bonnet as though playing a game. He scissors his legs out-in, out-in, and lets them hit the fender of the car. Baba Rakhu pulls the lid off the icebox, removes a weighty butcher knife from it and waves it in his hands. As the blade glides under the streetlights, the knife delivers light to the face of the chair-man. His eyeballs glint and dart. His watch catches the same light; it is time.

"I will go for the right arm. We will leave the legs intact since they are skinny. No one wants to buy skinny legs," says Baba.

If Baba Rakhu can paralyze by pressing nerve endings, make a man speak the truth by nipple adjustment, surely he can gracefully detach an arm. But that is the illegitimate comfort I seek. For once, when I need to most, I am incapable of dismissing what is real.

"Kindly hold your arm out at a right angle," Baba tells the chair-man.

The man suddenly extends his right arm. The fool thinks he is directing traffic.

"Isn't it convenient?" asks Baba. "No shrieks, futile begging and pleading, unnecessary rise in blood pressure. Look at him now, calm and fresh as a lotus on the water."

It is true. Even though the chair-man has not shaved in days, even though his hair is oily and feet rough-skinned, and the rim and strap of his cheap watch are lined with dirt, his face exudes the quiet of a faraway light blinking in the night sky.

Without warning, Baba raises the knife above his head and brings it down on the chair-man's arm. A cut cleaner and smoother than can be felt. But which (and appropriately) the chair-man now feels. He who was a little boy in the attic with his wife-doll has suddenly become a man. His cry is so curdling, it prevents the blood from spilling off the bonnet onto the tires. As my skin turns inward to check out my insides, I see his arm on the bonnet of the car — the fingers curled a little, the thumb pressed onto the forefinger to hold the stem of a rose.

"The loss of blood changes the balance," says Baba. "He is back in dishonesty mode now."

The chair-man tries to communicate. His speech is erratic: inside him has opened a Hindi dictionary and he is sporadically quoting words from it, words that bear no relation to his present situation. As he slowly slides down the front of the car, smearing blood all over, Baba drags the chair-man's pants down to his knees.

I look away. I look at the closed ration shops, at the mosque in the distance, at the faces of politicians slapped onto the walls, at the stall of the coconut seller, at the open-air garbage dump, at the car we came in, its steering wheel, its seats, its trunk.

I look back.

Baba has the chair-man's meat in his hands and dismembers him, as though he is eliminating a stale piece to be fed to the vultures.

"Now he is a true eunuch-dog," says Baba. "Part of the cash sale from this arm goes to his wife."

The chair-man's recital of synonyms continues. By now his eyes point upward. Mine are bathed in fear. Baba puts the knife into the icebox without wiping it. He lifts the arm from the bonnet and runs his hand over it, as if it were a child lost in an underworld of sewers and dead dogs.

THE NIGHT TRAIN

We leave the car behind at the taxi stand. I try to take my eyes off the icebox Baba carries. The road ahead is dug up. Telephone wires lay exposed. I can hear the conversations of people as I stare at the copper that holds the words of their lives. They are all lonely. They keep talking about it. I do not think Baba hears them, for he walks with the urgency of a man who is late for office.

At night this city is an old person inching toward the bed or bathroom. When there is light, there is pretense. The man who sells combs will say that he is no sadder than the man who sells fish, who will insist that he is as happy as the man who works in the bank, who swears he does not envy the man who owns it. But when light leaves, they all wail. This city knows that once it has gone to the bathroom and then to bed, only death remains.

I know we are near the railway tracks, for I can hear a train pass by. Its slow speed tells me it is a local train that stops at all stations. There is wild grass around me; we must be between stations. You cannot catch a train from here, but this spot is very useful for throwing yourself in front of the train. A few years ago, policemen were stationed here to prevent suicides, but then one day the policemen killed themselves. This city does that to us all.

"Look down and walk," says Baba.

"Why?"

"Fried éclair."

"What's that?"

"Fresh shit. Looks like pieces of fried chocolate."

"But it's so dark. Impossible to spot."

"Use your nose, fool."

"I'd rather step on fried éclair than smell it."

Those policemen must have killed themselves on account of the smell. Their lives and jobs must have brought them despair, but the smell must have driven them to jump before the train. I wonder if they had fried éclair on their shoes before they died.

"The train will come soon," says Baba.

"I'm not killing myself," I say.

"Fool, no one wants you dead."

"Then why are we here?"

"To catch a train."

"We are between stations. The train will not stop here."

"Not to worry. I will catch it by the neck."

I look around at the shrubbery. There could be all sorts of animals in there. Or small men who live like animals. It happens: you look at a small or medium-sized plant and wonder how it has feet. Why does it lie on the ground uprooted, shivering even though it is not cold? Then you realize that it is a man, or a child, or a man-child who slept on the earth so much, he has become a part of it and needs to crawl rather than walk, wither rather than die.

"Get ready," says Baba. "Our train is here."

"I have never caught a running train. I won't be able to climb on."

"It will slow down for a few seconds. You must climb on."

"For what?"

"Do as I say, cripple."

The train does slow down. It almost comes to a halt, and Baba lets the icebox get on first. Even though he is old, he boards the train with the eagerness of a runaway schoolboy. He helps me get on. The train picks up speed once more as we escape the smell of fried éclair.

"How did you know the train would stop?" I ask.

"The driver's family and friends board the train from here so they can travel without a ticket."

"Is that why we boarded? So we do not have to buy tickets?"

"We boarded because I need an empty compartment."

I look around and notice that there is only one other passenger in the compartment with us. He is a thin young boy. His head rests against the wood of the seat and his eyes are closed. The wind causes his white shirt to balloon. There are ads for mutual funds above his head. Also a caption for Tortoise mosquito repellent, a picture of the sturdy Atlas cycle, and the new mango soft drink that will cure us all of summer.

Baba opens the icebox. I know that no mango soft drink will emerge. He holds the arm in his hands. Dark hair has stiffened on it because of the cold. Drops of dry blood have settled on the crushed ice. Baba holds the arm at the wrist and points it to the night sky. He brandishes the arm behind him like a spear and flings it far into the sky. It flies away from us like some vicious bird.

"Why did you throw the arm away?" I ask in disbelief.

"I was about to ask you the same question."

"What?"

"Why did you throw *your* arm away?"

"I don't understand."

"You must retrieve your lost arm."

"Stop the train!"

"*That* arm is already lost."

I look for the arm, but it has flown. I am sure I did not see it land, but I know it *has* to land; it cannot just become part of a flock of migrating birds.

"The arm can't disappear into the skies," I say.

"Look at your arm," Baba says.

I look at it, but I do not know for what. My other one looked just like it.

"No," he says. "Not the one you have. Look at the arm you threw away."

"I did not throw it away."

"Is it there?"

"No."

"Do you know exactly how you lost it?"

"No."

"Then it disappeared? Just like the one I threw?"

"Yes . . ."

"So earn it back."

The train slows down again. Baba jumps off into the shrubbery, leaving the icebox behind. I am afraid to follow him. I do not think I am meant to.

"Throw me the icebox," he shouts.

I am happy to get rid of it. I push it off the train. I do not want the boy in the compartment to see the blood. I lean out of the train. I see Baba pick up the icebox and run back toward where we came from.

Then I understand. That arm was not for me, after all. Baba will retrieve it and sell it to someone else. Or maybe it did fly off into the skies. Either way, it does not matter.

Inside the compartment, I take a seat opposite the small, frail boy. His body is simply a hanger for his white shirt, which still puffs up because of the wind. But there is something else. He is not breathing too well. His chest heaves. His eyes are still closed. He must be flying kites or spinning tops with his friends in his village. Why did you leave your village? This city has eaten up half your body. The soul it took long ago.

I will wake him up. His station must have passed. I will ask him if he wants to eat vada-pow or even if he would fancy going to a proper restaurant. But it is almost midnight. All the restaurants must be closed. I have not eaten. This boy is not breathing properly. But his lungs are bold. They demand air and will not stop until there is none left on this earth. As I reach to touch him, I pause, horrified. Before I know it, I am calling out Viren's name. There is a pretty blue schoolbag in my hand and I want to thrust it upon this small boy's chest and crush his lungs forever.

***

The usual group of bad boys sits at Lucky Moon. We have our own little table in the corner, near the kitchen, far away from the sugarcane machine and its flies. The sugarcane machine has been replaced by a new one that is semiautomatic. It churns out the crushed shoots much faster. It is perhaps the most expensive machinery in Lucky Moon. The waiter has just put in a fresh batch of sugarcane. I watch as shoots of cane go in cylindrical and hard, and come out as pulp. It is a sophisticated process. Now that

I have been expelled from school, I would not mind working as a sugarcane crusher.

We are celebrating my expulsion from school by having cuttings. I am not too happy but I do not let that show. I play along and proudly display my beating marks to my friends. Mr. Old was mad, I say. See this mark. It is at least an inch deep. Even a horse cannot bear that kind of beating. We clink our tea glasses together and I watch the steam rise slowly. I want to say that I did it on purpose, that I hate Viren the sissy. But I do not. It is okay to lie in class, but not at our own table in Lucky Moon.

Irani Uncle calls to us from behind the counter. You boys keep an eye on things here, he says. I am going to the bathroom. If customers come, just say Irani Uncle is coming back very soon. Make them sit. Give them yesterday's paper.

Okay, we say. We come here so often that Irani Uncle leaves us in charge instead of the waiter, because the poor fellow cannot speak English and that drives away the occasional foreign tourist. (They come here by mistake.) As Irani Uncle leaves, I walk up to the counter and look outside. Suddenly I want to greet people on the street and invite them for a cutting like the owners of those posh cafés in other countries.

I do not know if it is luck, or fate, or simply a matter of Irani Uncle's bowels reacting at this particular time, but I see Viren near the school gate. It is his first appearance in a week after I hurt his eye. I look at him and decide to let him go. Let the English textbooks destroy him. Let the sissy be. He will grow up and still be a boy.

But then I want to know if I have brought him blindness. As Mr. Old would say, I wish to know the extent of my horrific act.

I go down the three white stairs of Lucky Moon. It is lunchtime and everyone is out deciding how to spend their lunch money. Cigarettes are a must, along with mangoes. For nourishment it is either a vegetable sandwich or a plain chutney sandwich. I weave through the white uniforms with blue ties, red ties and green ties until I reach Viren and his yellow tie. His blue bag is on his back and his eye looks fine. A deep gash near the eyebrow has been stitched. Mr. Old was scaring me. The boy is not blind. Upon seeing me, Viren turns away but he knows that in this crowd he cannot run far. So he turns back and faces me.

"If you even touch me, I will shout for help," he says. "All the seniors will hit you."

"Viren," I say. "I did not mean to harm you."

He is more afraid now than ever. He knows that I am sincere and it scares him. It is an odd feeling for me, too.

"Sorry does not make the dead come alive," he says.

"I never said I was sorry. I just want you to know that it wasn't on purpose."

"Did the desk come down on its own?"

"No, but I did not know about the nail. The nail was a mistake."

"It doesn't matter. I never want to see you again."

"You won't," I say. "I have been expelled from school."

I do not think he noticed I was in playing clothes. That is what I call anything that is not a uniform. We cannot play in uniforms because uniforms are meant to keep us tied and unhappy. I am happiest when I play. Even drinking cuttings is play for me.

"Mr. Old expelled you?" he asks.

"I bring shame upon his school," I say.

He does not say much. I think he feels bad. He should not. I should, but I do not. I do not feel happy or sad. School meant nothing to me, anyway. It only made me appreciate my playing clothes more.

"How about a cutting?" I ask.

"What?"

"A cutting. Have tea with me."

"No."

"Why not?"

But I know the answer. If I feel out of place with Shakespeare, Viren feels even worse in the presence of the likes of me at Lucky Moon. He knows he does not belong and that makes him feel stupid. So, in turn, he thinks it is stupid to have cuttings at Lucky Moon. I can feel his mind working, wondering what it would actually be like to sit in those magnificent surroundings and drink chai. His mother would hate it. He has never done anything his mother hates. This is a great opportunity for him. I make it easier for him by begging.

"Please," I say. "I'll feel better."

"But I want you to know that I'm not your friend."

"Viren, we can never be friends. But it is what men do. They have cuttings even though they don't like each other."

I lead Viren through the uniformed seniors with cigarettes in their hands. They keep the cigarettes hidden by their sides, as if they are holding guns, so the teachers do not notice. Why bother? The teachers smoke, too. We should have a smoking period in school and talk about the joys of cancer. For the first time, students and teachers would have something in common.

There are a few girls at Lucky Moon, adventurous ones whose mothers do not send them to school with food from home. These girls in their short skirts flirt with the seniors, sharing mangoes while the boys dare them to share cigarettes as well.

We enter Lucky Moon and the bad boys at our table are shocked to see Viren. Andha Kanoon has come, they shout. *The blind law.* They are talking about the fact that Viren is as good and straight as the law, and as blind. This is a Hindi movie reference and Viren does not get it. He does not watch Hindi movies; maybe Shakespeare told him not to. He looks down at the sugarcane machine. Perhaps the dirt and flies are spoiling his imported leather shoes. Irani Uncle is still in the bathroom and the waiter is in the kitchen preparing more tea.

"I'm going," says Viren. "This place is for fools."

"Have a cutting with me. Then you are free to go."

"Free?" he asks. "What do you mean *free*?"

That is how I talk. It was not a grand statement. Viren begins to lecture me and my friends in a loud voice. "If you have any brains, none of you will waste time here. Drinking tea all the time and coming last in class. None of you can spell. Besides your bloody address, what do you know to write?"

I do not know what has gotten into him. The bad boys get up from their table and walk toward us. I want to protect Viren for a change because I know he is an idiot. He is learned, the worst kind of idiot. Then I look at him for a second and a rage I cannot understand comes over me. Why did I allow this fool to spoil my school life? I should have the right to wear a uniform. My uniform should not have been taken from me. I have the right to own it, spit on it, jump on it, and then wear playing clothes instead. Why is Viren *not* blind?

I grasp his hand and put it in the sugarcane machine. I press it down hard with the shoots of cane. Before Viren can move, the machine eats his fingers. He screams and the bad boys do not move. I do not move. I look at Viren and wonder why he is so stupid. I want my school uniform back. I will feed it to this sugarcane machine just like Viren's hand.

My hand is shaking and the train moves faster. The small boy seated opposite me looks very scared. But once he notices that I am more afraid than he is, once he sees that the only arm I have is like a tree limb vibrating in a storm, he reaches out toward it. I want to tell this small boy that I am sorry. Even though he is not Viren.

"Did you just see a ghost?" he asks.

His hand is cold. He waits for an answer.

"I think I did," I say.

"I knew it. Your face is white."

"I've not slept in a while."

"You must sleep. Otherwise you'll see more ghosts."

He lifts his hand off me as though he has just given me a valuable piece of advice. Perhaps he has. The more hours I am awake, the more I awaken the past.

"I must go home," I say feebly.

"That's a bad idea."

"Why?"

"No one ever gets sleep at home. Why do you think I'm sleeping on the train?"

"Is it allowed?" I ask. The thought of sleeping on a train embarrasses me.

"Just choose a spot and go to sleep."

"But where does this train go till?"

"It's a local train. It won't go too far. Now make your bed."

I look around. All the seats are wooden planks that have been painted green. Some have nails sticking out of them; those I shall avoid. The small, round fans above us make a lot of noise but do not circulate any air. How can they? Their covers choke the blades, smother them completely.

But the boy is right. I may be able to catch some sleep here. I will catch it by the neck and force it upon me. Let it scream and shout. I will show it no mercy. This night shall bring me the sleep of a hundred happy children.

I realize that I have already broken the main rule of sleep: I have thought about it so much that I am now wide awake. The boy has already leaned his head against the window and dozed off. To prove he is an expert at falling asleep, he snores loudly, announces his sleep from atop a mountain with a blow of nose trumpets.

I walk to the end of the compartment, where there is an advertisement from the government in favor of safe driving: "If you drive like hell, you will reach heaven." I run my fingers across the green wooden seats to check for nails. I am satisfied. The boy's trumpet snores have steadied down to a soft whistle.

I rest my head on the hardness of wood and stare at the ceiling of the train. It is the cleanest part, no doubt. White as chalk. Just as I think this, I spot a crack. Then another. One by one, lines appear in the ceiling of the train, as if the train is aging right before my eyes. I look to my side and the green wood of the seat has turned into a green bedsheet. I am no longer on the train. I try to get up to confirm this, but *she* does not let me.

"Where do you think you're going?" she asks.

I stop putting my shirt on and remain naked. She is up on her elbows and her black hair teases the green bedsheet by hanging just an inch above it. I am still too drunk to speak clearly.

"I asked you a question," says Malaika.

She stares at me with dark, angry eyes. The sleep in her eyes is no match for her anger. She looks even more beautiful when she is upset. I do not think she will ever look old and wrinkled. I hate how she sits by the mirror and always looks beautiful. It is as if nothing can touch her, even though men ravage her by the hour, and leave their day's hopelessness inside her. Admiring her beauty is like staring defeat in the face.

I try putting my clothes on again. I am unable to find the right hole for the right button. The room is swimming before my eyes. I must drink some more to calm myself down.

"I'm going because you have work to do," I say.

I know it bothers her when I make jokes about her *hard* work. She finds it childish. So do I.

"No one's coming tonight," she says. She puts her head back on the bed.

I want to make another joke about no one coming, but I decide against it. I love this woman. But I cannot tell her that right now. I must buy flowers first. From now on, Malaika shall comb that long black hair of hers without being paid to do it. No man will be allowed to ask for the beauty of her mounds. No man except me. I am going to ask her to marry me.

"Please don't go," she says. "I've kept this night for you only."

"I wish I could," I say. "But I have an appointment."

"At this time of night?"

"It's in another brothel."

I say it with a straight face, and she buys it. I know this because she tries too hard not to let her hurt show. Her lips tighten, her smile hardens and she stares straight at me. Now, if she praises herself and puts me down, I will know that I have hit a nerve.

"Then go. Perhaps you need to taste a bad woman to appreciate an apsara."

It worked. She will be shocked when I ask for her hand. And her whole body. And the air that surrounds it.

I throw some hundred-rupee notes on the bed and kiss her softly on the head. It is the first time I have kissed her head. Her skin is hot and her face is turning red. We are already having husband–wife arguments. I love it. We will be so happy.

I climb down the wooden stairs and hope that someone is selling flowers at this time of night. I walk out in the street and things are dead. I am not referring only to the rats. The air is dead, the cars are still and a few beggars stir in their sleep. Only the music from the temple streams softly into the night. I walk toward it. It is a Sai Baba mandir. As the bhajans play, Sai's face looks serene. The music comes from an inner room — a midnight aarti must be in progress. I wish I had been born in Shirdi during Sai's time. He cared for dogs and people alike, and shared his wisdom with all men. I hope he will shed some light on me tonight.

There is too much alcohol in me. But I am not the kind to stammer and stagger. There is only one way to know that I am drunk:

You swim in my bloodstream and realize that it is not blood that you are swimming in. Maybe it is not a good idea for me to have another drink. I want Malaika to know that I am completely in control of my emotions.

Right under Sai's idol is a garland of flowers. White and yellow petals tied to a string. They smell fresh. Someone must have placed them here not too long ago. It is a sure sign that I must marry her.

After we get married, Malaika and I will go to Shirdi and take Sai's blessings. She will give up prostitution and I will give up drinking. We will not live in this city, though. I am not willing to have her spotted on the street by the hundreds of men who have taken her. The very thought makes me burn. Maybe marrying her is not such a good idea after all. What will she do? Does she know how to cook?

We could buy a house by the sea in a village somewhere. What if she has hidden talents? She could be a gifted artist and she may not be aware of it. I will buy her all the colors of this world. She will paint our house, the grass and bougainvillea around it, and even the sea. Then she will swim naked in freshly painted water, and I will join her. We will get a dog. A stray dog. We will live in Goa. We will drink feni (I cannot abstain completely) and dance till the sun comes up. I cannot believe I am thinking about dancing. How dreadful. I am in love. Children. Yes, four or five. I have finally lost my mind. Lots of children, so that they all shout and scream and fall down and we hear more shouts from the ones inside her belly, waiting in line, trying hard to burst out because we are such good parents. Then we will grow old and watch them get married. But they will leave us someday. Malaika and I will stare at the sea as it darkens, as the last of our children leave. We will be terribly sad, and I will ask her to paint the sea but she will ignore me and stare at the sea in silence. I am already sad. Life just does not allow us humans to breathe.

As I stare at Sai's idol, I ask him to forgive me as I am about to take the flowers that are meant for him. But what will he do with flowers, anyway? He is probably in another universe, blessing galaxies, turning planets on his palm, bending down every now and then to whisper bits of wisdom into the ears of this earth. I take the garland and walk out of the mandir before someone spots me.

I walk back to the brothel. The night does not seem dead anymore. Everyone is sleeping but their dreams are wide awake. People are laughing, singing, bouncing off the buildings, flying into each other's arms and kissing their own hands, because for the first time in their lives, they love themselves. Tonight I am able to love myself only because I love another.

As I climb up the old wooden stairs that lead to Malaika's room, a rat escapes into a hole in the wall. I can still see its tail; it makes no effort to go in fast. I must be like this rat, and stay shameless and rooted even if I am spotted trying to escape. I look at the garland in my hand and know that I will have to convince Malaika that this is not just the hotness of a mood, or the desire of a spineless swan.

I expect to see her seated by the mirror, looking as if she has just created the earth. But she is not. Nor is she sprawled on the bed, ready to allow passage to all of man. I take the green sheet off the bed, knowing that no man will ever lie on it again. I walk to her mirror and throw water over it, straight from the steel glass on her dressing table. She will prepare herself only for me from now on, in front of a mirror that only I pay for. I pull down the calendar that has initials and times neatly written under dates. Then I hear the sound of her moaning from the kitchen.

The garland withers on its own. One by one, white and yellow petals break off the string. Malaika's voice breaks as well. It trembles, it soars, and then it careens out of control like a drunken car. All I can do is stare in the mirror. I thank myself for throwing water over it so I do not have to see my face. Finally, I leave the room.

Outside, the rat is still trying to get into the hole. Its tail is shorter. It has moved in a little, and I realize then that it is not shameless. It is begging the walls to let it in so that it can turn its back on this world.

On the street, it starts to rain. I walk till my feet ache, but I know it is not really my feet that are hurting. I throw the garland to the ground and walk toward a parked taxi. I want to get home as fast as possible. I see a small boy seated under the roof of a ration shop, trying to escape from the rain. He holds the ends of his shirt out before him so that it serves as a bowl. In it I see a few coins. I stand in the rain and watch him. I cannot walk an inch farther — my heart does not allow it. Every minute or so the boy walks out into the rain and lets water collect in his shirt bowl. Then he sits down and stares at the wet coins. I do not know what it means, but it is horrible.

I stay there in the rain with the little boy and at first I want to give him money. I have plenty of it in my pocket. But it is of no use. It is raining and it is of no use. So I want this boy to die. No one must use a shirt as a bowl. I no longer feel sorry for the boy; instead I feel a sincere disgust. It is the most honest feeling I have ever had.

I imagine the man back at Malaika's place pounding into her again and again as if she is not real, as if she makes sounds on demand. Her moans are not real. They *cannot* be real. She must be acting. It is part of her job. She did not use the bed. She was in the kitchen. Perhaps the bed is only for me. But how can she moan like that? I want to tear my ears off. She enjoys herself only with me. With other men . . . how can there be other men if we have already bought a house in Goa? What about our children? I cannot let them hear her moan. No wonder she was sad and staring at the sea when they left. They left because of her. They heard her shouts for help and mistook them for cries of pleasure. I must save her. The only way to do that is to ask her to be honest. She will give me her truth and I will give her mine.

I run up the stairs. If her visitor is still there, he is a dead man. His body will be floating in the sea. Not in Goa.

I do not see the rat. There is the smell of beedis. He must smoke beedis. She cannot love a man who smokes beedis. I climb two stairs at a time, my heart losing count of how it hurts. I want to know who it is that makes her voice soar.

When I enter, she is sleeping on the bed with one hand over her face to block the light from the street. When she hears me, she lifts her arm away but does not get up. She looks at me as though nothing has happened, as if the night has not been torn apart. Although I had removed the green sheet, she has put it back on.

In my head I keep hearing her voice rise, as if I mean nothing, as if the counting games we played were just games. I should have stayed and heard her climax again and again, so that with each sunrise I could go sick and yellow with fever.

"I took the green sheet off your bed," I say.

"It's time I increase my rate."

"Did you hear what I just said?"

"No."

"I threw water on your mirror, also."

She looks outside, across the street to where clothes hang and movie posters have heroes with thick, black hair and full hearts.

"Say something," I say. "Please."

"There is nothing."

"Malaika."

"That's not my name."

"What?"

"That's not my name."

"Malaika is not your name?"

"It's my prostitute name."

"You have never told anyone your real name?"

"Not you."

When the heart leaves, the hands take over. At that moment, all these hands can do is transfer defeat to someone else. They pound again and again, upon that woman with no name.

THE EUNUCH & THE NIGHTINGALE

The small boy I met on the train turned out to be a wise old man. He told me that sometimes trains do not know when to stop. They get confused and keep going round in circles. Finally tracks come loose on their own and all passengers, like it or not, must wander off. So when morning came and the train was still moving, I got off at the next station and wandered off toward Chor Bazaar, of all places.

At Chor Bazaar you can get anything and everything. After all, it is created by thievery. You will say it is wrong to buy from here, it is encouraging robbery, that if you do not patronize this place, thieves will have no one to steal for. This attitude of white light continues until you find the one thing you have wanted all your life. You stare at it until every drop of water leaves your body. Then you buy it. Everyone buys it, you will say to yourself. As if one person can make a difference.

At Chor Bazaar you get Bibles that are two hundred years old, paintings of the Rani of Jhansi in the blood of her husband, and Gandhi's first pair of glasses. And if you know the right people, you can get elves, black magical witches and Jesus trapped in a wine bottle. It is not stupid to hope that I will find the arm Baba threw away. After all, he told me to retrieve my lost arm.

It is Friday today, the day thieves rest or branch out into salesmanship. They have worked hard all week, including Sunday, and now have the goods to show for it. Chor Bazaar is where they can display their credentials.

I walk through the silverware section. Bowls, spoons, knives, forks and ladles are laid out on an old maroon carpet. The owner rests his elbow on a silver coffee table. The owner's beard is dark red. He watches me intently and strokes his beard, pulls it lower and lower, and fine-tunes it into a sharp point.

"Silver like this is not to be found even in Saudi," he says.

"Saudi is known for oil, not silver," I say.

It is important to be chatty, to portray learnedness, otherwise bargaining can be hard. The tongue must be oiled and ready to go, prepared to slip in that last-minute halfhearted offer. If the tongue is dry, it will halt after every word, and you will end up buying manure.

"Oil?" he says loudly. "Ha!"

"How much?" I ask.

"For what?"

I do not know. I ask out of nervousness. The redness in his beard is too forceful. It makes me speak without thinking. "This table?" he prompts.

He taps the silver with his knuckles.

"That table looks good," I say.

"It is original."

Original what? What does it mean when they say that? This table is original. This pencil is an original pencil. This horse is an original horse. How can there be any other kind?

I look around me and see people on their way to the mosque. Perhaps the mullah has made the call; the prayer will start soon. The mullah's voice will rise, and with it, the mosque. It will float in the sky and emit colors — shades of moons, tamarinds, horses, swords — all praising the glory of God. It is said that a mullah's prayer can reach the ends of the earth. Light can travel with all its mighty speed, but a mullah's call will walk and still get there faster.

"No," I say. "Let the table be."

"I have something else," he says.

The mosque is light green, and sunlight hits its dome and sets it on fire. People have collected at the entrance and are exchanging greetings. They are polite and quiet. This busy street becomes a flower bed during prayer time. Then it resumes its quiet murders and nonchalant rapes. It is the way the world is now. When God is watching, love all men. When he is not, love the woman by your side, even if you do not know her. Force your love upon her like a constitutional law.

"I have a silver spittoon," he says.

"I don't chew paan."

"But you will still want the spittoon."

"For what? Show?"

"And what a show it will be."

He fine-tunes his red beard again. A man selling foreign underwear shouts at the top of his voice that he has only one more unused pair left.

The owner of the silver crawls on his knees toward me. He can only come a short distance, as the silver forks, lined according to size, operate as a fence between us.

"This spittoon was owned by . . ."

He bows his head down. Darts his eyes from left to right like a cat.

"What's wrong?" I ask.

"Quiet."

"Sorry."

"This spittoon was owned by . . ."

"Yes?"

"It was owned by . . ."

Once more he says it was owned by . . . and stops to admire the scenery, I will drain all the red out of his beard.

"Emperor Akbar!"

Even the owner is confused. He did not utter this name. Did the words come from the mosque? No. I look behind me and even the mosque-goers are looking our way. They have heard it, too.

"Emperor Akbar!"

The shout is getting louder, but I cannot see who is chanting the name of Emperor Akbar. I notice a line of scooters parked against a shop selling fireworks. The owner's beard is now candle-wisp thin, such is his concern.

A form tears through the men in white outside the mosque. Long hair wild, sweat on a face of dull, dark earth, and orange bangles on thin wrists. The sari is old and blue.

"Emperor Akbar!" he exclaims.

The stranger bows before me. It is not good that he thinks I am the Emperor. Mosque-goers do not like amusement during the slot reserved for the one and only. I agree with them. Religion is not funny.

"It's me, Horasi," he says.

"Horasi?" I ask.

"Don't you remember me?"

"No." I truly do not.

"I am your favorite eunuch."

He takes my hand, kisses it and leaves a neat deposit of spittle. "Dear Emperor, you will be pleased to hear that I can sing again," he says.

"Who is this Emperor?" I speak with the voice of a scared wind.

He launches into song. His head turns upward, toward the hoarding of Marie biscuits. His song has no words. It is an exhibition of tenor, tremor and terror more than anything else. He is awful with a capital rhinoceros. I am sure his voice will never reach the hoarding. Ugly things cannot fly. I can feel his voice hovering near my ankles like dirt and rainwater.

"Shut up, eunuch!" says the owner of the silver.

"Stop singing," I say. "You will be beaten."

"My king, you who have wiped out armies with one utterance, you who . . ."

The owner rises from his maroon carpet. His name must be Haroon. (It rhymes with maroon.) Now his face is also red, trying to contain his anger, trying to keep his blood at a flowable temperature.

"You must pardon me, my king. But I have to kiss you," says Horasi to me.

"What?"

"On the other hand, as well. It is the custom, my king."

"I don't have another hand," I say.

Horasi puts his hand to his chest. "Hai ray," he says. "You lost your hand?"

The mosque-goers come closer toward the silverware stall. It is not to buy spoons. The owner senses fighter-cock feathers in the air and decides to become as spotless as his silver.

"Eunuch, this area does not like your kind," he says. "If you come here again, we will cut your balls."

"But I don't have them," says Horasi.

"Chal nikal," says the owner to Horasi.

"Leave," I echo.

I can hear the mosque-goers ask each other: Who is the cripple? Why is a eunuch calling him Akbar?

"I'm not Akbar," I proclaim.

"My king, I can recognize you anywhere," says Horasi.

"This cripple is causing trouble," says the owner to the mosque-goers. "I did not trust him the moment I saw him."

Life decisions are often made in split seconds. The bottle lid remains open for very little time. Some djins make their escape; others live inside glass forever.

So I start running.

Away from the mosque-goers, over the maroon carpet and its silver barricade, past the scooters lined against the fireworks shop. Let them eat Horasi the eunuch for breakfast. Let them feed him to pie dogs as pie. I do not care.

As I run, I breathe in and out like they do on TV, those strong black men striding toward a white line. (They must make the tape black, for it is rarely a white man who crosses it first.) I shoot around the bend, where the road opens up into the animal market. I stop and look back. I hear shouts, loud *ya's*, and I start running again. The mosque-goers are chasing me.

Of all the things they teach you in school, very few help you. Even fewer can be used in real life. And most often, these are the things you have been taught incorrectly.

Never look down and run, they say. The ground is not running away from you; you are running *on* it. Take my hanging brinjal, I say to that! When in this city, look up at the skies for vegetable peels and fresh phlegm from building flats; look straight ahead for cows and other holy objects; look to the sides for places of escape; look behind for justified killers; look down for uneven sidewalks and mango peels.

I missed the mango peel.

I was taught only to look ahead. But in life or otherwise, do not look ahead. Look back. If you want, even look down in shame. Train yourself not to expect godly horizons and sunlit balconies. A positive outlook is a torn pocket. Whatever you put in it is lost when you enter the streets.

A half-eaten mango will lead to my death. It is not the bravest way to go, being beaten to death shortly after a eunuch.

Flat on my back, eye-levelled with a rotten mango, I do not get up.

"Quick, get in here!" Horasi's face looms over me. He could have been a dusky woman.

"You escaped?" I ask.

"I am a lowly eunuch. They are after you, my king."

"Where are you taking me?"

"Teahouse."

He helps me up and I smile at a woman who carries a cot on her head. She is probably taking it for repairs. I limp and run past the group of wholesale cardboard merchants who have found my fall amusing.

We enter Café Gulab, a kabab place. Yellow Formica, white Sunmica, unwashed glasses and tasty food. Horasi still holds my hand—luckily the café is empty. There are no gulabs here, no roses red in the face with anger. I jerk my hand away from him.

"Follow me," he says. "You will be safe, my king."

"Will you stop calling me that?"

"Yes, huzur."

"Where are you taking me?"

"Teahouse."

"Aren't we in it already?"

"This is a café. The teahouse is more inside."

Just then a man comes out from farther in. He is not old, but weary. His face wants to touch the ground and never get up.

"Just in time," the man says. "Your hookah is ready."

I look at Horasi, who looks behind us to see if any mosque-goers are near the café. If it is time for the prayer, they will ignore us. Allah has saved us. Prayers do save lives, even lives that are worthless such as mine.

"The coal was beginning to get cold," says the man.

"What coal?" I ask.

"Did you not order sixteenth-century coal an hour ago by telephone?"

"That was me," says Horasi. "For us both."

The man leads us into a green room with a small black table against one of its walls. There is a couch as well, also black. There are embroidered paintings on the wall: a beautiful maiden walking in air with the clouds below her feet; a lanky man with a diamond beard leading his sheep into a mountain. There are orange sweets in transparent showcases lit with tube lights to keep them warm.

"We must sit here," says Horasi.

"Look, who are you?" I ask.

"I told you. I am your favorite eunuch."

"What do you want?"

"You will enjoy the hookah."

"I don't want the hookah. I'm worried about those people outside."

"Those outside people will look at the empty Café Gulab and leave. They do not know of this teahouse. That is why we must stay here."

The weary man places a hookah on the black table. A long rope, green-yellow as a snake, coils toward us with a silver nozzle attached to its end. The transparent glass cylinder that holds water is slightly yellow from age. Bubbles rise as the man inhales a mixture of the coal and tobacco that burns atop a tiny funnel. The piece of coal is small; it will burn fast.

"We must go back, my great ruler," says Horasi.

"Out there? You must be mad."

"Not out there. Back."

I look behind me. There is only a wall.

"Into the past," he says. "The very distant past."

"Who are you? Has Baba Rakhu sent you?"

"Take one dum. All will be clear."

Horasi hands me the coiled snake with the silver nozzle.

"Take it fast," he says. "Keep taking till it goes to the head."

I greedily suck on the nozzle. There is the sweet taste of apple in my mouth. I am about to take my lips off the nozzle to exhale, but Horasi urges me to carry on. The taste of apple is now so strong, it must have been the apple plucked for the first woman from that first tree. The coiled snake I am holding in my hand confirms this. The lights illuminating the sweets become brighter and the orange sweets acquire a golden hue. Horasi's hair stretches out the entire width of the teahouse. It touches the clouds at the feet of the beautiful maiden walking in thin air. I take my lips off the nozzle and everything is watery. My eyes, Horasi's, the sweets, the clouds have become liquid, too. My head goes back and faces the ceiling with its chandelier full of rubies and diamonds.

A MIRROR OF SIXTEENTH-CENTURY COAL

The rubies are so pink, pink itself will stare in disbelief. The diamonds are very bright, but do not hurt the eyes. As the sun comes in, they reflect light that sweeps the whole room. I look outside through the arched window and see all sorts of parrots in the tree. Green parrots, blue parrots, red and violet wings fly through the leaves. It is a view fit for a king. The bed I rest on lets me sink into it until I am enveloped in white silk. I pick up a mug of red stone and drink. It is last night's sherbet. There are easily more parrots than leaves in that tree.

"At last you're up," says a woman.

She walks in with a tray and picks up the mug and a few peanut shells from the table. She is superb and has more wings than the parrots. She must be a queen. Only royalty can cast away mountains with charm. But why waste her delicate touch on trays and old sherbet?

"So how does it feel to spend the night in these chambers?" she asks.

"No different than most nights," I say.

I use my arms to rise from the bed and brace myself for her beauty. She smiles at my answer. Maybe we did something special last night and I cannot remember. This sherbet must stop. It is mad-dog flavor.

"My queen," I say. "I must eat. My head hurts."

"Juka, wake up."

"Juka?"

"You only had one night here."

"I'm hungry. Get me sweet nightingale."

"Cook it yourself. It's what you do best."

The king cooks? But I should be out in the world destroying tigers and elephants. "One more large feast seven days from now," she says. "If you cook like you did last night, Emperor Akbar will make this guest chamber yours."

"Emperor Akbar?"

She shakes her head and starts pulling the silk sheets from under me.

"What are you doing?" I ask.

"Changing sheets. The Emperor has guests coming from the land of strong rivers."

"*I* am your strong river."

I pull her toward me and she lands on top of me. No parrot can match this beauty, even if it speaks twenty languages and follows all religions.

"Juka!" she shouts. "To your own sister?"

"Sister?"

"Don't say I'm not your sister. Every time this sherbet enters your mouth, your brain leaves."

"I am not the king?"

"Of fools," she says. "Now get up!"

The silk leaves me and I feel the harshness of the woven cloth below. I must act in the proper way and find out what is going on. Why did I think I was king? That sherbet maker has played a joke on me. I will have him flogged. As a cook, I must surely have power over the sherbet maker.

"You have to be in the king's court very soon," she says. "Or have you forgotten that also?"

"I know," I say. "But for what?"

"Go and wash up. You look like a thief."

I leave the guest chamber and walk through the corridor. On the floor there are chests of dark wood with metal carvings on their lids, and in the walls there are heart-shaped holes to let the light in. The floor is white marble; it is cold as the rivers of the north. I look back at the woman who is my sister, whose hands are fairer than the silk she holds.

"This sherbet has taken your name away from my lips," I shout at her.

"Good. You'll stop calling me, then."

"Where must I go now? Left or right?"

She slaps her palm to her forehead once more and points to my left. I take the next left into a larger corridor with more wooden chests. The holes in these walls are crescent moons. Sunlight passes through them and onto the marble floor. Even when the moon is not real, it is a thief.

I walk fast and as I let the cold marble wake me up, I run my hands through my hair and comb it back. I lick my tongue all round my mouth and swallow the stickiness of the night's sherbet. My white robe is clean. I have no doubt I can cook. I am sure of that, even though I do not know why. I am also sure of something else. I have an enemy. My heart is a jealous stone that wants to hurl itself upon him.

We all stand and wait for the Emperor. I know most of the faces here: the jester, the wise man, the chief of army. Only men are gathered; no women. Everyone seems to know me and treats me as an important part of this court. Two strong men, bare of chest and long of hair, fan the empty golden throne. The usual conch is blown to announce the king's arrival and all our eyes fall to the floor. The bowing of heads is as organized as an army's slamming of spears to the earth. Even though we cannot see him, we know he has entered. The air stops breathing in the presence of our king.

"I will speak," says the Emperor.

The silence becomes even heavier; its legs are crumbling under the weight of the king.

"I must leave for the desert today. There is talk of a cowardly attack on our kingdom. Talk I can ignore. Cowards bother me," he says.

As he speaks, I feel my heart burn again. The stone is ready to be flung, but not upon our king. My enemy is here and my heart will lead me to him.

"I shall leave three thousand men here to protect my people. My army shall go with me. May God spit on us through our travels."

There is an audible gasp after his last words. The court is shocked by the inauspicious words of the Emperor. But I know he is wise and respectful. He is a shrewd king who likes to tease his subjects.

"I ask you all to join me in my humble request to God."

"But janab," says the wise man. "Do you think it is wise to bring down a curse from God?"

He is the only person allowed to speak in court without permission. I do not think he is wise. I pity him. He cannot be my enemy.

"Where am I going?" asks the king.

"To battle. It is why you need God even more."

"Who can tell me why I have asked God for this curse?"

I step out of line, as I always do, and bow before my king. I do not lift my head until I am given permission.

"Juka," he calls my name.

"My Emperor, may God spit on you a thousand times," I say.

Even though they are not supposed to, the courtiers shuffle their feet. They fear mine will soon be cut off.

"Tell us why you wish this upon your king."

"The Emperor is going to the desert. If God does not spit on our great Emperor, he might die of thirst."

There are claps and pats on the back, soft *wahs*, loud *wahs*, fake *wahs* and one or two genuine ones.

"The Emperor will miss Juka," says the wise man.

He is just an old fool who will soon go blind. It does not matter what he thinks. But I wait for the Emperor's reply.

"He will," says the Emperor.

"But who will the Emperor miss most?" asks the old fool again.

Perhaps he is not such a fool. He is trying to instigate something.

"Ah," is the reply. "Do I love Juka's food and wit, or will my love of song prevail?"

So song is my enemy.

"Will Horasi not sing for us?"

Horasi. It is a man's name. It is familiar. I do not like it. It starts with an H and ends with an I. H for Hate; I for an eye.

A song lifts toward the murals of the palace ceiling and the courtiers part ways and sit on the floor. A lone form in a blue sari, with long hair and orange bangles on thin wrists, is the object of all eyes. If the parrots in the tree are blue, his sari is bluer. If the parrots in the tree are red, so is my anger. But his song continues to rise, toward the picture of Akbar the Great killing elephants. Horasi's voice sits on the ceiling and looks down upon us. It is on Akbar's horse now, and travels from one mural to the next. Akbar towering over men like a tall god, Akbar blessing the poor with the palm of his hand, Akbar bringing the elephant he killed back to life. It is the most beautiful sound I have heard and, like all beautiful things, it must be destroyed.

When Horasi ends, Akbar gets up from his throne and walks toward him. Toward this person of no gender, this third person, who invented himself by default, who came in third even though only two seats were created.

"Yes, I shall miss Horasi the most," says the Emperor.

"Then why not take him with you?" I ask. It is not my place to speak, but I will take a chance.

"And risk losing him? Do you wish to be flogged?"

Horasi, seizing this moment, uses it like light from the sky. "But I will be ready to sing even if it means losing my life," he says.

"There will be no need. But there is a need to punish Juka."

"But my Emperor," I say. "I did not mean take him physically. There is a way for his voice to reach you."

"How is that?"

"Let Horasi sit on the highest dome of the palace. Let his voice travel over pink rivers, blue trees and orange groves if it has to. It will reach you in the desert and soothe you."

"Will Horasi do this for his king?"

"It is already done," says Horasi.

He looks at me and I look at the murals. There is no doubt that the stone in my heart is meant for him.

"For this great service to his king," says the Emperor, "I appoint Horasi in charge of my kingdom until my return."

"But a eunuch in charge?" asks the wise man. He could not have worded it better.

"Anyone who disobeys Horasi will answer to me. After they are dead."

"I must take my place on the dome this instant," says Horasi. "If I start singing now, my voice will reach the desert by the time of your arrival. Your horses are swift and strong, and I must keep up with them."

Horasi walks out of the palace, out into the rose garden of seven scents, past the fountain of golden water, into the tower that will take him to the highest dome.

And so the days pass like marbles on a steep slope, one after another, fast and changing colors. Horasi the eunuch sits on the dome and sends his song to the desert. He eats there, sleeps there and cries there; such is his devotion. From all across the kingdom his blue sari can be seen fluttering in the breeze atop a white dome like a martyr's flag. He is fast becoming a hero and when the Emperor returns, my food will taste of salty stone when compared to the sweetness of Horasi's desert voice.

Horasi issues orders. We must treat eunuchs as equal to men;

we must make little boys who are like girls *into* girls; we must weave saris of such length that they touch the palace grounds from the dome when he wears them. Such excess leads to a land's worst enemy; such indulgence leads to famine.

When the drought finally hits, they all come to me, for I am the greatest cook. I will find ways of bringing food to life even if drought has killed it. And they all go to Horasi because he issues the orders. Against Emperor Akbar's wishes, in light of the terrible plight of the kingdom, it is okay to kill birds for food. All birds can be killed, except nightingales — they are birds of song. That is the decree of the eunuch.

It is sad the way men plot their own defeat. But then again, Horasi is not a man. If we are not meant to die a natural death, nature will provide a way to bring one's downfall. The famine is nature's gift to me. And Horasi's gift — that of song — will soon leave him. Then even the fan bearer will be of more use to the king.

Past the garden of seven scents, behind the fountain of golden water, there is a tree. It is an ordinary tree, probably the most average one in the kingdom. It would have been cut and made into a wooden chest if it were not for the nightingale that spends hours in it. It sings every day, sends sounds of love and futile yearning far into the land.

I watch it sing now as I stand behind this ordinary tree. I see Horasi on the dome, his arms reaching far into the sky, invoking rain; his head is arched backward facing the clouds, his mouth is open. But I do not hear his voice, for it is somewhere near the orange grove right now and will soon cross the pink rivers. It will then reach the desert and the Emperor's ears. Horasi must fail.

I scale the tree easily. The nightingale does not know fear, for it has never been hunted. It thinks I am its friend. I slowly place my arm on the branch and move to its end.

One more day passes and the marbles are rolling faster. But their colors are weak. They have no power to change and do so slowly, bleeding into one another. The famine is strong and soon we could all be dead. But I will die a happy, vengeful man.

I carry two small morsels on a tray. They are the bird's heart and throat.

I stand at the foot of the dome and look up at the flying Horasi. He is hundreds of feet high and yet his sari rolls on the palace earth comfortably. I pull it hard and wave out to him when he looks down. The tray in my hand makes the sunlight climb the palace's outer walls.

I shout a little, but not a lot. When words are important, they reach the ears of those for whom they are meant, even if they are rivers away.

"I'm sorry for what I did, my king," I say.

My words travel upward like tiny soldiers scaling palace walls.

"I am not your king," he says.

"In the absence of the Emperor, you are. I offer you a token of peace."

Before he can reply, I wrap the tray with the nightingale's throat and heart in his long sari. I tug at the sari to signal he must pull it up.

"It is a parrot's heart and throat," I lie. "It will bring speed to your voice."

"Then I must eat this for Emperor Akbar," says Horasi.

When there is a famine, hunger overtakes common sense. When the stomach growls, so does the heart. It laps up wood and poison with the same delicious tongue.

I wave to him, walk into the garden of seven scents and inhale. On any other day, there would be the smell of warm sun, of sloping wind just fallen from the mountain, of strong horse and gentle cow. But I detect only one scent today: of blood leaving, of a voice becoming softer and softer.

If the bird of song is eaten, all men shall hunger for music forever.

The garden glows like some cheap stone. It rises and looms above my head, waiting to descend upon me. It comes lower and lower. Something is terribly wrong. A hand touches mine and pulls the hookah away from my lips. There is water everywhere, but it is receding.

I feel shame and look at the face before me. My enemy smiles at me. We are back in the teahouse at Café Gulab.

"Sixteenth-century coal is the best," says Horasi.

"Why did you call me Emperor Akbar?" I ask.

"Should I have called you my greatest enemy instead?"

"I took the gift of song from you," I say. "Forgive me."

"It is why we eunuchs have bad voices even today," he says. "Are you going to ask us all for forgiveness?"

"That will take lots of time."

"Yes," he says. "And you hardly have any time left."

"For what?"

"To earn your arm back."

"You know about the arm?"

"It was used wrongly," he says. "But you will soon begin to regain its wisdom."

"Why are you helping me? I poisoned your throat with a sweet nightingale's meat and killed your voice."

"I'm helping you because I need to atone as well."

"What did you do?"

"I cut off your arm in return. Or did you not get that far?"

"What must I do now?"

"Correct your past," he says. "Before it's too late."

VIREN HIERONYMOUS D'SILVA

The past is a tricky thing. You spend the present trying to forget it. So perhaps there is no such thing as the past because it is always present.

Viren Hieronymous D'Silva. With a name like that, it was easy for me to find his address. The phones in this city rarely work, but the phone books always do. Viren Hieronymous D'Silva lives in a building by the sea at Napean Sea Road. I am taking a taxi from Chor Bazaar to his house. I wonder if Viren Hieronymous D'Silva is married. No, who would marry the poor creature? Another poor creature, perhaps? It makes me sad. Two poor creatures living by the sea, staring at the water each morning, not knowing how unfortunate they are.

I must stop this. I am here to repent.

I do not know if he will recognize me. It has been years. The last time I saw him he was looking into my eyes as the sugarcane machine ate up his fingers. Perhaps he will remember my eyes. But I will not be able to look into his.

I knew even back then that what I had done was wrong. As Miss Moses used to tell me so often: There is such a thing as a line and you, my friend, have crossed it. Miss Bardet, on the other hand, had no wisdom to give. Whenever I did or said something indecent/immoral, she would have the same reaction — her breast would heave up and down and she would look around the room to seek confirmation from the walls, the fans, the desks, the chairs. Did the boy really say that?

God bless both those old birds.

I am very close to Viren's house. No matter where I go in this city, it is always struggling. The church to my left has a statue of Jesus outside. Below it sleeps a tiny boy, curled into a ball, remembering the days when he was warm in his mother's womb. Behind the church is an old Parsi mansion, built during the British rule, which will fetch truckloads of money when sold. But the man who lives in it lives alone, separated from his family, drinks his tea with a shaking hand and curses his daughter as he wonders why she married a bloody car mechanic.

One day this city will burst. There will be so much sadness it will be unbearable. Waves of misery will sweep the neighboring countries as well. We will all drown together, holding hands, being laughed at by the rest of the world. Only in death will we know that we could have been friends, helped each other by burying our nuclear weapons in our deserts until they were forgotten. We have brains, we have guts, but we have left our hearts under the huts of the poor.

Too many new cars have cropped up. They look like tiny colorful boxes that have been painted by children. Most of them have a small accident within the first week of purchase. It is a sort of initiation to the city. When I was little we only had the Standard Herald, the Fiat and the Ambassador. The Mercedes, of course, has always been a part of this city. People cannot afford to eat or shit, but they have a Mercedes. I had one, too. But I could eat *and* shit. If you are poor, you keep the food in your system out of fear. You do not let it escape, because you do not know when you will get your next meal.

I am right below Viren's building. It is sea green, although the sea looks dark brown. What will I say to him? Will he even recognize me? He will smell me. There are certain smells you pick up in your childhood that you carry with you for the rest of your life. For me it is the smell of fish. I shall forever associate it with the silence between Mother and Father at the dinner table. I wonder what I smell like to Viren.

I walk toward the lobby of the building. The sea breeze is warm and wonderful, like the laugh of a child. There should be more seas in this world. Fewer boats, though — they eat the laughter of children.

As I look up at the name board to find out what floor Viren lives on, the lift door opens. An old man totters out. He needs a walking stick but looks too proud to use one. Let the fool fall and break his teeth.

Viren lives on the seventh floor. Seven is my lucky number. Actually it is everyone's lucky number. I am simply avoiding contemplation of my meeting with Viren with thoughts like these. It is like a trip to the dentist, or minor surgery. It has to be done at some point.

Years ago, after the accident, I thought of writing a letter to Viren. I call it an accident because although it was done on purpose, it was not premeditated. My mother taught me that. In her formal, boring lawyer voice she asked me, "Did you plan on crushing that boy's fingers?" I loved how Mother never called anyone by their name. Viren was *that boy*. My father was *that man*. Even her lover was *that judge*. "You think I'm having an affair with *that judge*?" It broke my heart to tell her that I saw him atop her, a fat man trying to mount a mare, clumsy, panting, looking around to see if he was making a fool of himself. Anyway, I told Mother I did not plan on hurting Viren. It had just happened. "Then it was an accident," she told me. So even though Viren's parents complained to the police, my mother complained to *that judge*, and the police dismissed it as an accident. My surgeon father kept performing operation after operation. At home he cut himself so much while shaving, it looked as if the Pakistani government had tortured him. But I did think of writing Viren a letter.

Because I was expelled from school, I had tutors come to my home. They were told that I was a disturbed child. I never thought of myself as disturbed, but then, a mad person always thinks he is normal. It is the normal ones who eventually go mad.

I enter the lift. The overhead fan blows my hair a little. In the small mirror, I watch my face. New lines have appeared and my eyes look hollow — like my shirtsleeve. I press the number 6. I shall walk up one floor in order to tire the shame and fear that I feel. I hope Viren recognizes me and slams the door in my face.

I get off on the sixth floor.

As I climb up the flight of stairs to the seventh, I say a short prayer. It surprises me, for I have never prayed in my life. The prayer comes right from the center of my being and I send it out-ward, upward, to heaven. For the first time, the absence of my arm is filled by something lighter: mere thoughts, but positive and powerful, God's very own war tank.

My fingers shake as I ring Mr. D'Silva's bell. It is midafternoon. I hope no one is home. The door snaps open and I am surprised. That was too quick. Did he know I was coming?

A beautiful woman stands in front of me. Her hair is wet. She must have stepped out of the shower. She is lovely. There is nothing else I can say. She notices that my mouth is open but no words come out. As a result I feel even more awkward, obliged to speak.

"I have the wrong address," I say.

"Who are you looking for?"

"Viren D'Silva."

"Oh, Viren. He's at his desk. You must be from the newspaper."

Before I can tell her I am not from any newspaper, she has already opened the door wide to let me in. I look down at the ground and enter. I am sure she must have noticed my hollow white sleeve.

"He'll be out in a minute," she says.

"Okay," I say.

"You don't seem to have a pen and paper," she says. "How will you conduct the interview?"

"I . . . I'm not from the newspaper."

"Then who are you?"

"I'm Viren's . . ."

I want to say *friend.* For the first time in my life, I truly want to say that I am his friend.

"I'm from his school days."

"A school friend!"

She said it. Not I.

"Aren't you proud of him?" she asks.

If a newspaper wants to interview him, he must have done

something. Who would have thought Viren would have anything worthwhile to say?

"Your name?" she asks.

I remain silent. I am too confused to say anything. Viren is being interviewed. This lovely woman must be his wife. I am a cripple who has not eaten or slept much in three days. What went wrong?

"Oh, don't tell me. We'll just surprise him," she says.

"No . . ."

But she has already gone inside. My heart starts thumping. If I were a rabbit, I would hide in the kitchen and never come out. What am I talking about? Rabbits do not hide in kitchens. I look around the hall. There is a single wooden chair, a few Chinese vases and a large statue of the Buddha. Next to it is an oil lamp. The flame burns bright as if it is angry, protecting the house from something. My heart has not yet calmed down. This is what Viren must have felt every time I approached him. The damage I have caused his heart.

And then a man appears. It is hard to call him a man — he is so frail. Instead of looking at his face, I stare at his right hand. The fingers are missing. Except the little one. Why did the machine not eat his little finger? I cannot bear to look up. All three of us are silent. Maybe they are staring at my missing limb just as I am staring at Viren's missing digits.

"Hello, Viren," I say. I am unable to look up at him.

There is no reply. I still look down. You notice the oddest things during times of shame and guilt. I stare at my feet and notice that they look like those of an old man — wrinkled under the sandals I wear, afraid of going out in the cold. When I finally look up,

I have a feeling Viren has recognized me. I know this because the woman is gone. He must have sent her inside. All I needed to do was say his name and St. Bosco School must have swum before his eyes, along with the dead-rat water, his pretty blue school bag, the sound of girls laughing, him wheezing and the pain of the grinder crushing his fingers.

"How's Shakespeare?" I ask. What else can I say at a time like this?

Viren is very thin. His hands are long and hairy, and it looks as though his skull has been sucking his face from inside. He looks cancerous. I will not ask him about it. He walks to the wooden chair and sits down. There is only one chair in the room, so I continue to stand. Why was the woman so happy? It looks as if he is about to die. Ah, but it makes sense. If one person is sick, the other has to act super-healthy.

Viren takes out a cigarette from his blue shirt pocket and lights it. No cloud, no rain, and Viren is smoking. He was the type of boy who, if he had the money, would buy all the cigarette packets in existence to prevent others from smoking.

"What happened to your arm?" he asks.

I swear he is smiling. Behind all that sickness, there is a wry smile. I like it. He is laughing at my pain. It is not like him at all, but it is refreshing.

"I lost it," I say.

"How?"

"I'm not sure."

Surprised by my answer, a puff of smoke comes out of his mouth on its own. "Why are you here?"

I do not say a word. I look at him. There is a certain calmness about him. He is not afraid anymore.

"Who was that woman?" I ask.

"My wife."

"She's very beautiful."

"She's okay."

"What?"

"I won't be able to enjoy her for too long."

"Are you dying?" I promised I would not ask, but his remark leaves me no choice.

"I was dying, I'm okay now. But she's leaving me anyway."

So that is why she is happy. Perhaps she gets this house.

"Why is a reporter coming?" I ask.

"My novel won an award."

"You wrote a novel? About what?"

"Shakespeare," he says. "It's about how Shakespeare never wrote the things he did. It was a woman, Helen, a prostitute, who wrote all his plays. He kept her in a cage for years until she died."

His body is sick, but his brain has finally been cured. He has started to think like a normal person.

"You must go now," he says. "The reporter will be here any minute."

"But there's something I want to say first."

"Say it fast, then leave."

The doorbell rings. I look at Viren and he looks right back at me. Words are useless. They are rotten vegetables that no one should use. Viren gets up and thumps me on the back. He coughs and takes one more drag from his cigarette. I put my hand on his back, too. As we walk to the door, Viren goes to the statue of the Buddha and picks up the oil lamp next to it. Perhaps it is a peace offering. With my left arm, I hold his right hand. All he has is one little finger. I shake it. He coughs again. Something in his eyes tells me he finds it funny. His behavior is very strange. There is no malice in him at all, just a mischievous gleam in his eyes.

I open the door. The oil lamp is still in his left hand. The reporter walks in as I walk out. Viren takes a last hard look at me and blows the oil lamp out. I know I will never see Viren again. But I am happy. The boy I had harmed has become a man. I wish him well.

As I descend the stairs, instead of feeling light, my heart begins to burn. I do not understand this. Have I not been forgiven? But my steps grow heavier and heavier, until I am forced to stop walking. I try to lift my feet but I am unable to do so. It is as if someone does not want me to move forward. As I stay rooted to the tiles, Viren's face floats before me. It glows in the light of the oil lamp. In ghost form, his smile does not seem friendly now. I see him blow out the oil lamp, and then I am plunged into darkness. A terrible thought hits me.

I think of what the lady of the rainbow told me.

A sworn enemy will try and end your journey before it is truly over.

That bastard Viren has not forgiven me at all. That is why he kept smiling. He wants me to fail. That is why he extinguished the oil lamp. But there is no way he could have known about the thousand oil lamps. Thoughts run through my head like angels in a slaughterhouse. Each time an idea flies, tries to make sense, its wings are chopped off.

I must flee this place or I will be defeated. It has the negative vibrations of a murderer. No wonder I am unable to move forward.

Viren does not want me to complete my journey. If I cannot walk, I shall crawl.

I place one arm on the step before me and descend. Unable to bear the weight of my body, my hand trembles. My knees hurt and my bones ache. I must make it to the lift. I look at myself and realize that I am no longer human. In the end I am reduced to a trembling, crawling creature.

THE LOGICIAN

There are many things you still do not know about me.

For example, when I was little, Mother took me to see the Great Russian Circus. It was dull, very dull. There was nothing Russian about it. As we walked home, I asked Mother if she would take Father, climb to the top of a tall building and jump off. I would stand on the street and watch them fall. It would certainly be more daring than anything I had seen in the circus. She was disturbed by my question.

A few days later, we were at the dinner table. One of my cousins, a boy I had never met, had had an accident that very day. As Mother and Father ate their fish and vegetables, they discussed the boy's condition in the grimmest manner. The poor boy ran from a mad dog, they said, straight into a bus. It flattened his face completely. Upon hearing this, I roared with laughter. It was much funnier than the clown act in the Great Russian Circus. I told my parents what I was thinking. They stopped eating.

My point is this. If Horasi the eunuch wants me to correct my past, is it possible to rectify thoughts of this nature? Also, do I need to? Horasi also said that I must do this before it is too late. How much

I can correct depends on how much time I have left. The lady of the rainbow set the clock. If even one of the thousand oil lamps is still burning, I have time. But it is impossible to trace the oil lamps. Instead, I think, I must find out how much oil is left. It is wonderful how my thoughts have become so linear over the past two days.

I stand just outside Viren's building. My knees are skinned from crawling, and my white clothes smell of sweat and defeat. But I can walk now because I am out of his building. I look at the building opposite me. And then I stare at its name.

Rainbow Apartments.

Surely I will find someone there who knows how much oil is left. It is an old building, but its feet are strong. I count three floors. A few clothes hang outside the windows and collect dust from the street. The road is being dug up. No children live in this building. Either they have all grown up and left, or they were killed in a tragic accident during building renovations. Perhaps a slab of gray stone fell from the terrace and crushed them all. I think this because there are no children's clothes hanging outside. I also smell sadness — each slab of stone stores it like an old person stores the death of a loved one in his teeth.

I enter the building. The corridor is dark.

I have always heard people say that when you are in trouble, a door will open. I do not have that kind of time. So I must start knocking. A door will open only if it is meant to.

On the first door there is a sticker that says: "Where there is a will, there is no confusion about money." I knock on the door and read the sticker again.

The door opens. The woman who stands there must be in her forties and has big hips.

I blurt out: "I'm depressed. Life is too hard to bear."

"What?"

"I'm sorry," I say. "Did my eruption surprise you?"

"Eruption?"

"This sudden display of emotion. I'm not accustomed to it."

"Who are you?"

"You don't know me. But I think the future is bleak."

I can tell from the way her hand grips the door that she wants to shut it. I fall to one knee.

"It's all over," I proclaim.

"What is?"

"I cannot pinpoint. The issue lacks specificity."

"Get out!"

She slams the door shut. This is fine. A door will open only if it is meant to.

The door next to hers is of a similar dark shade. There is no sticker on it. I knock three times. The opener is short and stocky. His right eye is smaller than the left one.

"Your right eye is definitely smaller," I say.

"Who are you?"

"That's a hard question."

"Listen, what do you want?"

"I want to buy some time."

"Then stop wasting mine!"

"I was right. It's all over."

I look down dejectedly.

"What's all over?" he asks.

"Even the lady next door asked me that. It's strange how people in the same building think alike."

"You know the lady next door?"

"No. But I was telling her that it's impossible to define what's over. I could say the oil is over. But that is being too specific. Do you see what I mean?"

"You better get out of here," he threatens. "Before I make you."

I turn around and climb the stairs that lead to the next floor. I can hear the door shut behind me. Yes, his right eye was smaller than the left.

There are two doors on this floor, one to the left of the other. I must choose carefully now, be extremely logical: I like to play cricket. I am a lefty (batting only) so I knock on the door to the left.

As I wait for the door to open, I notice that the wood around the keyhole has scratches. There is the shuffle of feet, a thump against the door, and silence. I assume I am being inspected through the eyehole.

"Who is it?" It is the voice of a woman. Her accent tells me that she is not from the city.

"It's me," I say. "Open the door, I have something to tell you."

"Are you here for Madam?"

"Yes, I have a message for her."

A chain unlocks. A dusky young girl stands before me.

"A chain unlocks," I say. "And now a dusky young girl stands before me. But it is bleak, so bleak."

"Sorry?"

"Tell Madam that human existence is pointless. I could tell you that the oil is over, but that would be too specific."

I lie on the floor. The tiles are cold and dirty.

"Look here, I do not know why you are talking nonsense, but Madam is not at home."

"Can you help me?" I stare up at her.

"With what?"

"I'm depressed. Life is too hard to bear."

I hear the door being chained again.

I notice a crack in the ceiling. It forks like a serpent's tongue. I recollect what most men recollect when they stand at a serpent's tongue: two roads, A and B. A leads to a dark woman with one tooth. B leads to a dark woman with one tooth missing. Since A and B are at the ends of the fork, the two women do not know of each other's existence. They live in isolation. Since they live in isolation, they do not know the norm for teeth. I surmise: if the serpent's tongue was not forked, the two women would have known each other. If the two women had known each other, they would have known the norm for teeth. But would the dark woman with one tooth have given hers to the dark woman with one tooth missing? That is what makes everything so bleak. Added to that, the oil is over.

I hear the sound of a person climbing stairs. I assume it is a man because otherwise it would be a woman. It is impossible to decide whether I should get up.

"Hello." It is a man.

"Same to you," I reply.

"It's good to see that you are aware of things, lying down like that. Not many people know the importance of lying down."

"That's the kindest thing anyone has said to me all day."

"Naturally. I'm mankind."

"Then you will understand the bleakness. The bleakness."

"Get up and face mankind," he orders.

It is an ordinary face, quite featureless, like an unimportant plain on a map. A white cloth shopping bag is strung around his wrist; he wears blue rubber slippers. Their straps fork like a serpent's tongue.

He leads me to a third door. I am surprised to see it, since I thought there were only two doors on each floor. There is no key-hole. He pushes the door open with two fingers, using the same hand to which the shopping bag is attached. The shape of a small bottle is evident through the bag. The room is completely bare, as though it does not exist.

"Your slipper straps fork like a serpent's tongue," I say.

"They are roads that lead to two women," he replies.

"You know about the two women?"

"I do. It's very sad."

"Why?"

"The woman with one tooth did not give hers to the woman with one tooth missing."

"I must lie on the floor again."

"It's what dejected people do."

"Lie with me," I plead.

"I must not."

"Please. Lie with me."

We both lie with our backs on the floor and stare at the ceiling. There is no ceiling — no concrete, no sky, nothing. Mankind does not say anything. He places the shopping bag on his stomach. It clearly contains a bottle. He removes it, leaving the bag dangling from the wrist. Inside the bottle is a thick yellow liquid. Very little remains.

"Is that oil?" I ask.

"It is."

"So it's not over, then."

"This is all that's left," he says as he turns a little my way.

✣

If there is little oil left, the lamp is still burning. I must act fast. I have found my logician. It is not a good thing. I once walked into a room full of people who were smiling. They sat on chairs, on sofas, on the floor, and there was a disturbing sense of group joy in the room. I stood there fixated. They were brilliant magicians all of them. I asked, why is everyone so happy? One man coughed, a young girl bit her nails, and the remaining dismissed my query as though it was an inopportune request for ice cream. But they did not know why they were happy. When the magician meets the logician, the first crack in the sidewalk is formed.

SWIM WITH THE WILD HYENA

If Viren cannot forgive me, at least Malaika can. For I know she loved me.

The last she will remember of me is the beating, almost a year ago, but probably still fresh on her body. I will tell her that it is only fitting that I do not have an arm. I will tell her it was not her beauty that I loved. It was the counting games we played, the way she insulted me and laughed, the way her hips moved toward me each time I kissed them, until I wanted to die between their flesh.

I take a taxi back to Sai's mandir, near to where I last saw Malaika. There are many garlands around his idol today. At his feet there are rose petals, and someone has left a photograph of a little boy. I can tell from the picture that the boy is no longer on earth — he looks happy. When we die and go to the spirit world, our photographs on earth change; they acquire the peace of blue skies. It is still early for the evening aarti, so there is no music. The man who looks after the temple is in a corner, cleaning the pictures of Sai on the wall. I have come here to seek blessings so that I can win back my love.

It is not the right thing to do, visit a temple and then a brothel, but today I go to the brothel for unusual reasons. I go to save

Malaika and myself. Even if she does not want to be with me, I shall convince her to leave the brothel. I will give her money to buy a small house somewhere and paint. Why do I keep thinking she can paint? It must be her love of colors.

I do not know what else to tell Sai. I never loved Mother because she did not love me. Father, the shaving expert, was too well-mannered to say anything to Mother. Each time Mother made love to the judge, Father became weaker. In the end he was afraid of his own voice, and he died without a sound. He called me the night he died. He did not say anything over the phone but I knew it was him. The lines were never that quiet.

Mother, on the other hand, went out in style, shouting and screaming, telling the judge that he had ruined her life, that he was fat and stupid. How could he judge people when he could not even judge his own weight? She died shortly after Father, alone and unhappy just like him, but loud. The neighbors used to tell me when I would visit that she spoke a lot to the walls and furniture during her illness. She spoke to Father a lot, and she knew he was listening because when it was his turn to speak, everything would go silent. Even the clocks.

I think Sai understands. From what I have heard, he never lets anyone down. This street has not changed at all. Same rusty roofs, ration shops, old taxis and people who walk slowly because they do not wish to reach wherever it is they are heading. Just like me. Even though I have walked slowly, I eventually stand at the bottom of the wooden stairs that lead to Malaika's room.

I do not spot the rat today. Maybe it died, or found a permanent home in the walls. The stairs have not aged a bit; how could they when they were already old and creaking? Perhaps this is a bad idea. What if she is with a man? The door will be closed then. But why did she leave it open the night I last saw her? Did she want me to see her being consumed by someone else? I hear a crunching sound. My thoughts are eating my brain.

The door is open, but a white curtain covers the entrance. It is new and spotless. It looks out of place. I stand before it and prepare myself for her. The heart lets you down when you need it most. It starts crying for help; it begs me to get out. I tell it to shut up. It is spoilt and rotten and has been pumping too much blood to all my body parts. It needs to calm down.

I part the curtain to one side.

That is not Malaika. It cannot be. This woman looks like her, but it cannot be. The woman looks at least ten years older. Malaika's black hair was never this thin. The woman looks startled as I enter. Malaika, what has happened to you? You challenged men as they entered; you did not cower in the bedsheets like an old forgotten doll.

"Malaika?"

"I'm not Malaika," the woman says.

"Thank God." I should not have said it out loud.

"What do you want?"

"I'm looking for Malaika."

"Who are you?"

"Her . . . friend."

"Then you must be a real useless one."

"Sorry?"

"She's dead."

"What?"

"Like I said, you are a useless friend."

211

I look at this woman and want to pull out her hair, strand by strand, for lying.

"What are you staring at my face for? Either get your body on this bed, or get out."

"Where's Malaika?"

I run toward the kitchen to see if she is in there. Even if she is under another man, I do not care. I will watch her make love to a hundred men, but please do not let her be dead. Why is this woman lying to me? If she knew about our plans, about Goa, the house by the sea, the children, us painting the sea together, she would lead me to Malaika right now. But the kitchen is lying, too. It hides Malaika.

"Tell me where she is," I say.

"I told you."

"If you want money, I will give it to you."

"Malaika is dead."

"It can't be."

"I'm her sister. I should know."

No wonder she looks like Malaika. An older, defeated Malaika.

"How did she die?"

My heart starts thumping again, beating its head against the walls of my chest. She was alive a year ago. A year ago, her flesh was in my mouth. How can she be reduced to ashes so soon? All those nights of lovemaking scattered over the sea.

"She was beaten."

The woman's lips tremble when she says this. I understand now. My heart was shouting and crying outside because it did not want me to come in here and find out the truth. I turn around to leave.

"It happened a year ago. We suspect it was a regular client, a rich young fellow. She used to tell me about him. But we have no proof. I don't even know what he looks like."

"Are you sure?" The words come out cracked.

"He was drunk and hit her too hard. She died a day later. She used to love the bastard because he called her name all the time. It was a game they played."

By now, the only hand I have shakes so furiously, I have to hide it behind my back. The heart is pounding as if it wants to tear out of my chest and throw itself on the bed, next to this woman, so she can see how black it is. She continues to talk, but I am not listening anymore. I do not even know if I am crying. It is hard to tell. I do not see anything, except my hand coming down on Malaika again and again like a hammer that just will not stop. I must have hit her a lot. I must have beaten her till she stopped fighting. I do not even remember if she fought. All I know is that she was breathing when I left her.

❦

I spend the next few hours floating from one corner of this city to another. Even though it is night now, the sun beats down on me. People take off their clothes and burn their skin on purpose. God says it is my fault. I must apologize to all burn victims. I can hear his voice so clearly, it is that of an old, battered woman. I talk to the first person I set eyes upon. He does not respond, just looks to the sun as it eats up his skin. No one cares. In minutes we will all be reduced to smouldering ashes.

Little boys and girls sit in a row on the street and pluck out their teeth one by one. They strongly believe in the tooth demon. They have not eaten for days and he has told them he will exchange teeth for bread. The children seem quite happy with this barter. But then a girl, no more than two years old, breaks out of the line and tells the others that they must not trust the tooth demon. His plan is to buy *all* their teeth. Without teeth, they will not be able to eat. They will die. That is the tooth demon's plan. They all point to me and tell me my plan has failed. They collect the teeth they have plucked out and fit them back into their mouths.

I see Mother and Father sipping tea at the tea stall. They look like they are in love. Mother holds a razor blade in her hand and cuts Father's face again and again. Father stays very calm and reads the newspaper. His blood stains the paper, but Father says it is all right, the headlines are always bloody. After every cut, Mother dips the blade into the tea. Don't look so disturbed my son, she says. We're having your favorite — cutting. Father laughs. For the first time in his life, Father laughs.

I am now inside Mother's womb. My sister is with me. This is how I know Mother was meant to have twins. What happened? I do not want to find out. My sister says she loves me a lot. I love her, too. She talks about angels and I tell her how I killed twenty-seven giants in a past life. She laughs at me. She says I could never hurt anyone because I am too gentle. So to prove her wrong, I kill her right in the womb. Then I feel sick. So I take my brain out of my head and rub this incident from my memory.

Tonight I would like to tell everyone I have ever known that I am sorry. But they have all turned deaf.

MORNING SQUATTERS

I crouch at the bottom of a huge mound of grass and mud. It has the width and length of a tabletop and is close to the railway tracks. I am back at the fried éclair factory. I want to be like those dead policemen.

In this city, one minute you are in a garden and the next you are in a slum. It is most natural. Ask me to retrace my steps and I will be unable to do so. A person travels in this city like a bad smell — over here now, strong and pungent; then gone suddenly, only to reappear in another part of the city a few moments later.

It is early morning. I can tell you what I did for most of last night. I spent it right here, staring at the night sky, begging the darkness to stay forever. When light comes, it forces you to see things that are true. But the night never passes judgment.

Beyond the tracks is the underbelly of the poor, houses hand-built by husbands and wives, with stolen roofs, under whose heat run five or six children. Some are custom-made gambling dens where the little ones serve liquor and boiled potatoes to the card players. It is said that if a person who is not from these parts can drink the tap water and remain standing, he is strong, an iron stomach amongst gutless men.

Dawn is a funny time to be here. Dawn is the stand-up comedian whose only trick is falling down. When it comes, people do not laugh at its routine, but at what awaits them during the rest of the day: no cooking oil, a plastic sheet for a roof and the last medicine for the month. It is their false laughter that fools the comedian and keeps dawn coming every day.

"It's no use. It's impossible until the train comes."

The words come from the top of the mound. I crouch lower and hide behind the mud hill. I cannot show my face to anyone.

"What does the train have to do with it?"

The voices belong to two men who seem to be quite close to each other.

"It's hard to explain," says the first man. "You wouldn't under-stand."

"Maybe I will," says the second.

"Okay," says the first man. "Some people need a newspaper. Others need a cigarette. My uncle would make his wife stand out-side the bathroom to talk to him while he went. If she·left midway to do a chore or answer the door, he would feel lost and constipated for the rest of the week. But I don't have a wife like my uncle. He is ninety-three, but rich. Not like us, living hand to mouth."

"Andha, I wish you wouldn't say that."

"I knew you wouldn't understand," says the other.

"I mean stop using that expression, considering what function we are about to perform. But I still think your theory is rubbish."

"Has the train come yet? I'm dying over here."

"Then why the hell don't you just let it happen? It is destiny.

It is meant to happen each morning. What if the train does not show up? Will you squat all day?"

"Daru, please don't say that. Last week when the mill workers went on strike and lay on the tracks, the train did not pass for hours. Neither did I."

"Then get over this ridiculous habit."

I hear one of the men drink from a bottle. It is a desperate suck, a dying man's draw for air.

"Has it come yet?" asks Andha.

His voice is a drawl. It is slow: the words fall out of his mouth, crawl along the ground and climb up to the ears of the listener.

"Why are you craning your neck?"

I think I have been discovered. I get off my haunches and stand up. The two men are squatted on the mound, facing the other way. They are completely naked but are wearing slippers. A Dalda tin can is between them. Instead of cooking oil, it must contain water. There is a walking cane placed on the ground. I return to a semi-crouched position and peek like I used to when I was little and inquisitive. Even my palms are red, just like they used to be with paints and crayons. But I have blood on my hands now.

"What in the name of country liquor are you doing?" It is Daru.

"I'm trying to see if the train is coming," replies Andha.

"But Andha, you are blind!"

"I'm desperate."

"Maybe you need some liquor," says Daru.

"Is that your answer to everything?"

"The problem with the world is that there is not enough alcohol in people. That is why their health is bad. That is why our country is not the superpower it should be. Why do you think our country was technologically, spiritually, every-cally advanced in ancient times?"

"People were always drunk?"

"Kings, courtiers, maidens, wise men, even the gods."

"And then you ask me why you are poor. I'm blind. I have an excuse. You are a moron."

I hear a loud expulsion of gas. I cover my nose with my arm.

"There! I hear it," says Andha. "Is that the train?"

Daru looks down sheepishly. "I made that sound."

"You are a vile person. You have been brought up badly."

I see a kite in the sky. In the morning sun, it looks sad. One of the children must be flying it. There is a reason the poor fly kites. Years ago, when the first hut was built, a mother looked at her little son. He was glum, and so she made a kite for the boy. But he would not fly it until she explained the kite's purpose to him. She said he could attach his problems to the kite and send it to the sky. The Kite Master upstairs, if he so wished, could reclaim the kite and with it, the boy's troubles. That is why, contrary to belief, when a kite's string breaks, it is a good sign.

"Look," Daru says as he points to the slums. "I was born here. If I'm about to pass gas, what do you expect, a memo?"

"Pass me my cane," says Andha.

"Do you wish to move? Do you not like this spot?"

"Perhaps it's not the train. If we change our spot, I could go."

"That logic I'm willing to accept."

Daru maintains his squat, reaches out and hands Andha the cane. It is old, held together by duct tape. Before Daru can vacate his spot, Andha whacks him hard. The blind swing hits Daru on the shin.

"O! You could cause severe harm to my uncoveries!" he shouts.

"Then take the train matter seriously."

The kite is making me ill because someone else is flying it. Each time it goes higher, the Kite Master is plucking off someone else's problems. I will need to fly many kites before someone hears me. I must relinquish my other arm as well, for the Kite Master to notice. I will tie my arm to a kite and send it to the heavens. I will feel lighter with no arms at all. If I have used my hands wrongly, who am I to keep them?

I stand up behind Andha and Daru. I walk around the mound and appear on the tracks before them. Andha may be blind but he is rich in other parts. The alcohol has taken its toll on Daru. He is smaller than life.

"O hero, what are you doing?" shouts Daru. "The train will be here any minute."

"Who are you talking to?" Andha asks him.

"A young cripple with too much energy is walking along like it is his father's garden."

"Have some sympathy. Don't call him a cripple," reprimands Andha.

"He's walking on the tracks. When the train comes, the driver might stop if he spots this cripple. Sorry . . . youth."

"You bastard! Get off the tracks, you cripple! You one-legged biscuit," he shouts. "Daru, what is missing — arms, legs?"

"Left arm. But be sensitive."

"He must leave the tracks alone. Where's my cane? You one-armed bandit, I have to shit!"

I look behind me and the kite is still high. It is steady, the result of an expert hand. I cannot make out the color. It is dark blue or black. Sad kite, sad kite. I turn around and look straight at the squatters.

"He's looking at you," Daru tells Andha. "He's the rich type. They come to these poor locations when they are depressed. They feel like they are really suffering then."

"Is he staring at my . . ."

"Yes, we are a novelty for him."

Daru is right. Open air scares me, makes me conscious of how worthless I am.

I lie down on the tracks like a sniper, with my stomach to the ground. I extend my arm across the tracks in the direction of the two men.

"What are you doing?" Daru asks me.

"Waiting for the train," I reply. I adjust myself so that my arm is across the tracks.

"Good, even I am waiting for the train. What a fine young man you are."

"There's something wrong with him," I hear Daru tell Andha. They whisper.

"You're right about that," I confirm. "There has been murder."

"What does he mean by that?" Andha asks Daru. "Is he being literal? Or is it rich-talk for something? Like when they say they are really suffering, they mean their air conditioner is not working."

"Or when they say they are feeling lonely, it means they want to hire more servants," replies Daru.

Andha looks skyward. "May the train driver get syphilis! May his wife get syphilis! May his mother get syphilis!"

"I have a suggestion," Daru says. "If I make the sound of a train approaching, you might be able to go. What if it is not the physicality of the train but its sound that coaxes your bowels?"

"Daru, you may be right. I'm blind. I've never seen the train."

Daru does not wait for the go-ahead. He makes the sound of a train, softly at first, as if it is behind a mountain and is turning sweetly around the corner.

Now Daru's *chook-chook* sound gets louder.

"The train has straightened out and is aiming for us," he says. "The driver has seen us and knows we await him. His teeth gleam and his grip tightens on whatever he is holding."

Andha strains to pass something. "O . . . O . . . help me."

"Push, Andha. Push. Be a man!"

The sound is deafening; the train is only feet away from us. The train will take away my arm, tear it from me, and I will be happy at last. I will be able to look at the kite and feel nothing. I might even cut off my legs. Then ask someone to place me on the edge of a well and tip me over. I will make a tidy splash.

"Has the train passed?" asks Andha.

"By now the train has reached Pakistan," says Daru.

"I'm doomed. Even an imaginary train is not helping."

"Tell me, cripple, why are you trying to kill yourself?" asks Daru.

"I want to kill my arm," I say. "I don't deserve to keep it. I will donate it to the train."

"Why don't you donate it to Baba Rakhu instead?"

"What?" I ask. "You know Baba Rakhu?"

"Never met the man. But we've heard of him," says Andha.

"Isn't it wrong, what he does?"

"His selection is very fair. He will never take a limb without reason. He's a great man, a helper of the poor."

"How is he a helper of the poor if he charges twenty thousand?"

"You've already been to him?"

"Yes," I say. It is as though we are talking about a common dentist.

"You must be able to afford it. Are you rich?"

I nod. I look into Andha's blind eyes. It is as though glass has been shattered and blue ink poured into his pupils.

"If you are rich, can you buy me a train? Then I won't have to wait for one," says Andha.

Daru gets up from his seat and walks to me. He takes my hand. "Join us," he says. "There will always be time to lose the arm."

"I must lose the other arm," I say. "I don't deserve it."

"Never refuse a poor man's invitation to the bathroom," he says. "You might find the open air refreshing."

There is the sound of a real train.

"Joy to the world," says Andha. "I will be able to go at last."

"Join us," says Daru. "We like company."

Even though I resist, Daru pulls me up and guides me to my spot, between the two of them. I take my pants off but leave the shirt on. A naked man with no arm is perhaps in bad taste. Also, like Daru, I am smaller than life. But I have had my moments.

As I crouch, I begin to feel fortunate to have found these two men. They are gentlemen of the river, hats tipped neatly as the fish swim past. It is a privilege to sit here and watch morning come.

"You know," Andha says, "it's rude to face people on the train like this and expose our private parts. Let us be cordial for once."

"Let us turn around and save face," states Daru.

The three of us change direction on the mound. I will not have to see the faces of passengers, and children pointing out our ladyfingers to their mothers.

"You can start," says Daru. "You don't have to wait for the train."

"I would like to wait for the train," I say.

As the train passes, so do we. It is a glorious feeling to be in synch with other men. I can no longer see the kite. I hope the string breaks. I hope the kite floats away, and gets stuck in a tree.

MOSQUITO NET

Andha's and Daru's home is a tiny cubicle of a place with a low roof. We have to bend when we stand. At least we do not have to squat. It would be too soon to squat again. It is very hot and the same stale air keeps moving from corner to corner. There is a row of empty whiskey bottles on the floor. I am very careful not to touch them.

There are so many mosquitoes here that it looks as if the mosquitoes have formed a net to trap humans. They move toward me in some sort of army formation. Not a single one flies out of line or attacks me. They wait for the command.

"The key is not to resist them," says Daru. "The more you resist them, the more they will target you."

"Yes, if you ignore them, they will feel insulted and leave you alone," agrees Andha.

So I turn my back on the mosquitoes. It is a big mistake. They come for me. I slap my cheek several times. They also like the back of my neck. I can feel the blood being sucked out. A few big ones bite through my white shirt and gain entry to my stomach. I swat and keep moving about the room. But they have their teeth clenched into my flesh with determination.

"Stop moving," says Daru. "I'm getting motion sickness. Look at us. Are the mosquitoes biting either Andha or me?"

I look at the photographs of deities on the wall instead. They are framed in wood without glass. If I had to assign tasks to each of them, the man with the mace in his strong hands would be in charge of killing mosquitoes. I would also request him to club me to death.

"The mosquitoes leave Daru alone for health reasons," says Andha. "They are afraid of alcohol poisoning."

"And they leave Andha alone because he's blind," says Daru. "They will not attack those who cannot defend themselves."

I slap my thigh. I circle the room and flail my arm about in a cycling motion, as if it might be the appropriate and respectful manner of invoking the insect-god.

"I can't bear these mosquitoes!" I shout. "Do something."

Daru slaps me hard across the face. The man is small but not weak. I try to remain manly about it.

"Killed the bastard," he says. "The one with the malaria germ."

Andha swings his cane in my direction and it hits me on the right shin. "Direct hit!" he shouts. "That was a massive one, the leader is dead."

"Is that all you can do? Make fun . . ." I want to complete what I am saying but it is useless. It is too late to change anything.

"We could be serious and complain about the abject poverty we live in. Daru, would you like to hear about my misery?"

"It would be my pleasure," he replies. "But one minute."

From behind the row of empty whiskey bottles, Daru pulls out a radio. It is old and has a huge antenna, as I assume each mosquito has.

"We will need musical accompaniment," says Daru. He catches a station that plays classical music. The sound of a sitar pierces the stale air. It is a shameless attempt to generate fake emotion.

Andha throws the cane down and puts his hands together below his chin like paws. He wiggles his fingers and then starts clawing toward me.

"What are you doing?" I ask Andha.

"He's telling you his story," answers Daru. "In sign language."

"Why in sign language?"

"It's more touching."

Andha carries on. With each action it is clear he knows nothing of sign language. He lies on his back and parts his legs. "I was not born like this," he says, as he looks upward at the low roof. "What wonderful eyes I had. My eyelashes! They would flutter like a butterfly."

Daru cuts in: "I will translate. As a child, I was happy. Now I'm blind and sad." Daru walks to Andha, kneels on the floor, closes Andha's parted legs and consoles him, feigning grief as he hugs him.

What else can they do but make a mockery of life? It is only natural that in this country people believe in a hundred gods. One God is not enough. One God has failed them, so they invent their own and worship them with words, milk and flowers in the hope that at least a few of these gods will come to life and help. I do not think it is stupid at all. Let people in other countries laugh. They would not last even a day in this hut. The mosquitoes would peel off their soft skin while they wondered what happened to the toaster and dishwasher, and why the smell of fresh paint has been replaced with the smell of shit.

Andha gets up from the floor. "Did you like our story? Does it warm your heart and move you to mournful tears?"

"No," I say.

"Good. It's not your pity we need."

"I understand."

"We are poor and so we have survived. You rich ones are sinking and drowning all over. Now it's your turn to survive. Decide if Baba Rakhu is the answer. If not, all we need to do is move farther away from the tracks so that your blood does not splatter over us when you sacrifice your arm."

"Do you want to know a secret about your lost arm?" asks Daru.

"What?" I ask.

"It misses being with the other one."

Their hysterical laughter drowns the next sitar tune on the radio. The photographs on the walls are just photographs. They do not have the power of gods.

LIFE STORY

The transition from the mosquito hut to Baba's dungeon does not seem drastic. In the hut, mosquitoes came in droves and covered the walls like curtains. In this khopcha, limbs do the same. The limbs are safer. At least they do not suck blood. But it does feel odd to be in dungeon-darkness at breakfast time.

"I knew you would come back," Baba tells me.

"Why is that?" I ask, irritated.

"If you didn't, your life story would stop. Even if our lives stop, our stories go on. Our stories have already lived a few days ahead of us. They know what will happen. They tug us along and lead us places."

"And how do you know *my* life story?"

"I don't. But I know mine."

"So what am I about to do next?"

"There are three men. They like to drink tea, but they have no milk."

"No more riddles," I say. "The night has been long."

"How long?" He pulls an arm out from the display. "This long?" He indicates shoulder to elbow.

"No."

"This much?" Shoulder to wrist.

"No."

"An arm's length, then."

I nod.

"I shall keep you at arm's length until you catch up with your life story."

"Just tell me what that means. I'm too tired to think."

"Right now we are on opposite sides. Bring yourself onto the same side as me."

ARM'S LENGTH

I am back inside the mosquito hut. I am not unprepared this time; I have smeared my body with a green mosquito repellent. I need to be on the same side as Baba. Andha and Daru will show me how. Perhaps it is just my imagination, but I think the photographs on the wall have changed places. It could be a custom that I am not aware of. All gods are equal and must therefore be shifted around the room.

Daru is on the floor, back hunched, still stroking an empty whiskey bottle. Andha, blind vision on, is reading a torn and tattered book.

"How's the book, Andha?" asks Daru.

"Good photographs." Andha's cane is placed across his lap. He never uses it to walk; it is his toy. Andha drags his forefinger along the page. An inch higher and he will be reading thin air.

"Still a one-armed bandit?" Daru asks me.

"All limbs are sold out," I lie. "This city is on a limb-buying spree."

My repellent has the mosquitoes confused. Now they will be forced to attack the blind.

Andha closes the book. "You are destined to remain a one-legged biscuit," he says.

"I have lost an arm," I correct him.

"One-legged biscuit sounds better."

The photographs could have changed places on their own. After all, they are gods. If we do not pray, the gods get bored. If the gods get bored, they play games. At night they must be flying around the room, picking their own spots on the wall. Andha is blind; Daru is a drunk. Only an insightful cripple can catch them at their game. I want to spend the night here and see for myself. Covered by a blanket of mosquitoes, I will keep one eye open and check. If I am discovered, I will say that I am the one-eyed god, a new addition to their family. (They have no means of checking because there are so many gods.) I will catch the weakest and find out if there is a riddle-god. In this city you need a thick skin and a solver of riddles.

"Are you good at solving puzzles?" I ask Andha and Daru.

They look puzzled. They parley.

"I think it's rich-talk again," says Andha.

"He means his new car is eating up too much petrol," replies Daru.

"Or the silver teacup on his bedside table is unpolished. It can be quite traumatic if the rich cannot see themselves in silver."

"Look," I say. "All I want to know is if you can solve puzzles."

"We cannot," says Daru. "I'm thirsty. I need tea."

"Tea? Won't that spoil the liquor taste?" asks Andha.

"I want to quit," says Daru. "It's spoiling my career."

"Well, then," Andha says. "Make some tea."

"We are out of milk," says Daru. "Do you have milk?"

"No."

Daru points to me.

"No milk," I say.

"We are out of milk," says Daru.

It is not the mind that remembers words. It is muscle. It has to be. Muscles twitch, spotting a familiarity in vowels, sounds, the way words travel through the air in curves and spirals, reaching the ears of those for whom they are meant. My body has recognized something right now. The soles of my feet tingle as I think about Baba's words.

There are three men. They like to drink tea, but they have no milk.

"Do you both like to drink tea?" I ask them.

"I am a man who likes to drink tea," says Andha.

"I am a man," says Daru. "That is enough."

"Do you have tea here?" I ask Daru.

"No tea, no milk."

"Then we must go to the tea and milk," I say. "Where is the nearest tea stall?"

"It's a long walk," says Daru.

"Very long," echoes Andha.

"How long?" I ask.

Andha indicates his shoulder to elbow. "This long?" he asks Daru.

"No," says Daru.

"This long?" Shoulder to wrist.

"No."

"An arm's length, then," he says and looks my way.

GOONDA

The tea stall is just around the corner from the mosquito hut. It is small, a shelter for some poor animal during heavy rain. Three broken benches are scattered outside as though someone left them there in a hurry. A blackboard nailed to the entrance provides proper guidance to all customers. In handwriting that slants to the right are the following instructions in white chalk:

No Combing

No Singing

No Reading

No Standing

No Spitting

No Abusing

No Killing

I must bring myself onto the same side as Baba. Things that make perfect sense are false and should not be trusted. You must be illogical to understand the world. If I say a fish is out of water, you will say it is dead. I say, why pinpoint the obvious? If the sky is blue, you will say the day is clear; I say a beautiful angel has worn a blue gown and we are all looking up her legs from under it.

This tea stall is run by a tea girl. I thought all tea stalls were run by tea boys, *all* affectionately called Munna no matter how old they became. But this is a tea girl. Behind the small partition in the interior of the tea stall I see her head. Its sideways movement suggests she is washing something. I am glad we are here. I suddenly yearn for morning tea.

"Here we are," says Daru.

"Now buy the tea," Andha tells me.

"You order it," I say out of respect. "We are in your area."

"Sit on the bench. The tea will come," remarks Daru.

The bench rocks under our weight. When the three of us stop shifting, it settles down. There are benches but no tables.

The tea girl walks out with two steaming glasses of tea. She is no tea girl, but a full-fledged tea woman. She hands the glasses to Andha and Daru. She sweats a lot; must be the steam from her large pot of tea.

"What tea, Munni!" says Daru. "Class. Too good."

So all tea girls are called Munni. She has gone back in.

"What tea, Munni!" echoes Andha as he slurps the tea. He is quite loud.

"Etiquette," says Daru.

"Manners," says Andha. But his next sip is just as noisy.

I wait for my glass to arrive, but then trains are always late.

"Munni!" shouts Andha. "This pendulum is waiting for his tea. Hurry up!"

I hear a loud noise. I think I know what it is, but I am afraid to ask. Andha and Daru continue to drink, so I assume it is only a firecracker. They notice my concern.

"It's only a gunshot," says Andha.

"A gunshot?" I ask. "A real gun?"

"Yes, it must be Goonda," he says.

"Goonda?"

"Contract killer." Andha has almost finished his tea.

These impoverished men are casual. They are orange leaves falling on your cheek.

"Goonda is only coming for his tea. Why are you worried? You've done nothing wrong," says Andha with a wry smile.

"Have you?" Daru roars with laughter.

They know about Malaika. I am going to be punished for it, killed in a cheap tea stall. If that is the way I am meant to go, so be it. But I refuse to be afraid. I will have tea with the contract killer. It should be like having tea with anyone else. After all, he is not going to pour the tea in his gun and drink it.

A thin, sunken man sways our way. His silky white clothes and shiny black gun are too loud for the ruins that surround us.

"Killed cockroach, bad cockroach," he says to himself.

I want to tell him that the cockroaches, black and brown, are already dead. They have stopped coming to me. But before I can say this, he points his gun at us. I duck for cover and scramble underneath the bench.

"Get up, fool," says Daru. "That's his way of greeting you. Don't swing like a pendulum before he even talks."

Goonda stands very close to Andha and looks down at him. "You are blind, I am not," he says. "Munni, is tea in the pot?" he shouts.

He then greets Daru. "You drink liquor, I drink not. Munni, is tea in the pot?"

He lowers his gun and looks at me. "You are delicate, I am not," he says.

I cannot think of a single thing to say.

"You are delicate, I am not," he repeats.

Daru glares at me; this makes me even more uncomfortable. Goonda simply puts his gun to my head.

Click.

With the click of Goonda's gun, something clicks within me. I look at his arm and realize that his limb and digit, the opposite clutch, is the one that I must turn to the good. I must save Goonda's arm, because I was unable to save mine.

"You are delicate, I am not," he says.

"Munni, is tea in the pot?" I talk back.

He lowers the gun. "Pleased to meet you, I am not. Name is Goonda, contract killer, what?"

"I am armless, you are not. But I must save your hand, understand what?"

"Where did you find this specimen?" Goonda asks Daru. "From our area?"

"Yes. He's staying with us."

I can feel that Daru and Andha are proud of me. Their tuition has worked.

"Munni! Too long for tea," shouts Goonda.

Yes, Munni. You take too long. Even I have not had tea. As Goonda walks to the interior of the tea stall, I look at Daru for approval. I am sure this was a test.

"There's no bigger sinner than Goonda," says Andha.

I look behind to see if Goonda is out of earshot. He has disappeared behind the partition with Munni. They must be lovers.

"All sinners deserve to be punished," says Daru.

"We must go. We have a business meeting," says Andha.

I stand up.

"No, your place is here. Goodbye, friend," says Daru.

"You will soon be complete," Andha says.

There is a gunshot. I find it hard to breathe. My stomach muscles clamp and I clutch at a wound. The bullet must have gone in so deep that there is no blood. I fall to the floor. The bench is the last earthly object I touch.

"You idiot," I hear Daru tell me. "Just when we thought you had improved."

"Did Pendulum think *he* is shot?" Andha asks Daru.

Goonda casually sways out of the tea stall. There is blood all over his silky whites.

"Too long for tea," Goonda says. "So I sent Munni on a long holiday."

"Sinners must be punished. They must be prevented from doing more harm," whispers Daru. He and Andha walk away from the tea stall and toward their mosquito hut.

And then I finally understand. The solution is for Baba Rakhu to take away Goonda's arm so he cannot hold a gun. Even Goonda will become a eunuch-dog. We are on the same side now, Baba and I.

Goonda goes to the blackboard. With his silk sleeve, he erases the *No Killing* sign. I have found the lost arm. It is Goonda's arm, more lost than anyone else's. It is that of a trigger-happy boy, skipping through the marketplace, killing everyone simply because the morning sun is out.

I know it is time to return to Baba Rakhu for a final visit.

LAST LESSON

I do not know what to make of this city. Trees are few, men are many, smoke is mistaken for air, prayers are mistaken for threats and answered with blood. Colors rule our eyes: brown of water, orange of temples, green of mosques, red of bindis, yellow of heat. I wait for the black of Baba's dungeon to take over as I descend the concrete stairs into his khopcha.

Somehow it is quite light. A humble glow comes from below. It is only natural that in a place like this, a reversal occurs. Light overrules its own laws by emanating from the earth and traveling upward.

When I reach the bottom, the starkness of the room alarms me. A single arm hangs in the center of the room with the surety of a piece of meat on a butcher's hook. I was prepared for seventy, not one.

"Where have all the arms and legs gone?" I ask.

"I sold a few since we last met," says Baba.

"That was barely an hour ago. There's only one arm left in this room."

"Your eyes see only that which they are meant to."

He walks to the center of the room and stands directly under the arm. He looks at it from different angles with his own hands clasped behind his back. He is strolling through a mango grove, contemplating the ripeness of the last visible fruit.

"Do you recognize this arm?" he asks.

"No."

"You might if you observe its behavior."

I stare at the arm. Baba does not take his eyes off it, either. I am not sure what I am expected to note. I am no better than the village idiot who stood alone and watched the guillotine for hours, waited for the blade to slice even though no one was scheduled to be beheaded.

I position myself under the arm just like Baba has. It is slender, not bone-thin, and has hair only on the forearm. The wrist and bicep are clean. I feel very uneasy. It has a face whose name I cannot remember and I wonder if I should be calling out to it.

"Any idea?" he asks.

"No."

"Even after noticing its behavior?"

"But it does nothing. It just hangs there."

"Exactly. It is *your* arm. The one you lost."

"What?"

"All its life it has been good for nothing. So I took it."

"*You* took it?"

"In one clean cut."

"That's a lie. I can prove it."

"The photograph they showed you in hospital was not of your arm."

"How do you know about the photograph?"

"I took it."

I look at the arm that hangs in the middle of the room. There is no burn mark on it. Baba walks to the arm and pulls it down from the hook. He takes it out of its plastic sheet. It is coated with the oily substance for preservation. The hair on the forearm sticks to the skin. This cannot be my arm. There is no burn mark on it. Baba places his thumb over the bicep and rubs vigorously. As the oil starts to come off, a mark appears like the winning number in a lottery ticket. When it is fully formed, he stops rubbing and points it out to me.

"Is this what you're looking for?" he asks.

"Yes," I say.

"How did you get this mark?"

"I cut myself when I was little," I say. "On purpose."

I reach out to touch my arm. But Baba puts it back in the plastic sheet and hangs it from the hook once more.

"The only way you recognize your own arm is through a self-inflicted wound," he snarls. "That should tell you something."

"What right did you have to take my arm?"

"You asked me to."

"I gave you permission to cut off my own arm?"

"To cut off your past. "

I know what I must do. I will not buy back my arm. And nor do I wish to renounce the world and become a saint, or suffer silently like some poor village girl who views her sad reflection in a river. But I do want to go out with dignity.

"I don't want my arm back," I say. "Destroy it."

"What?"

"Burn it, cut it into small pieces, feed it to vultures. I don't want it."

"Are you sure?"

"That arm is my past. If you attach it, you are giving me back my past and I may return to its ways."

"Your arm may be lost, but you have begun to regain its wisdom."

"Then I must leave now. Before I change my mind."

"My dear cripple, you will *never* be able to leave."

"What?"

"You will work as my apprentice. When I die, this vast empire of limbs will be yours. You will carry on my work."

"You must be mad!"

"I thought you wanted to repent."

"I do."

"Then you must help others by ridding them of their rotten, misguided limbs."

"But we must end suffering, not add it."

"The world can be changed not by ending suffering, but by a more judicious distribution of it."

I look at myself and realize that he is absolutely right.

I will make a fine apprentice. Like I did with Goonda, I will spot sinners from a mile, for in their eyes I will see mine. Through their useless limbs, I will detect the familiarity of a lost, misguided brother. I will hunt them down. But the cutting I will leave to the master tailor.

"I accept the position," I say.

"But you are still not ready," he replies. "Bring yourself onto the same side as me."

"Baba, I thought I did."

"Take a look at your arm again."

"What did I miss?"

"It's not what *you* miss. It's what your arm misses."

It misses being with the other one. Andha and Daru had given me the answer, but I was too afraid to take it.

So I extend my right arm.

"What are you doing?" Baba asks.

"I must give up this arm as well," I say. "Take it."

"You want me to cut the other one off?"

"Donate it to someone who deserves it more."

"You have made me proud, my cripple."

I lie down on the floor, directly under the arm that hangs.

Baba towers above me. As I look at his beard, I realize that each hair holds the wisdom of the ages. He resembles the prophets of old, strict and unforgiving at first, but turning more and more human as time goes by. The blade of a butcher's knife gleams in his hand.

I close my eyes and wait.

Suddenly a strong wind starts to blow.

It is Malaika. She flies toward me in a golden sari that spans the entire sky. The wind blows her long black hair as she lands. She sits besides me and takes my head in her lap. Then she touches my face and looks down at me as if I am her only child. I wish I were paralyzed in this position for life. I beg her to take me with her. She opens her mouth and speaks in gold — of fire, and rain, and wind, and of all that is far away and that I must cross, streets and streets, deserts and deserts, before I get to her. Then she places my head back on the ground and leaves. The sky follows her.

I cry out to her: *Wait until I come. And don't even look at another man.*

She turns my way one last time and whispers: *Tonight when the stars come out, I will spray them with silver and then go blind.*

EPILOGUE

This city is a widow. It is always mourning a loss.

Songs pour from its walls, water taps, roofs and chimneys to blanket our heads and faces like a slippery veil.

A song is a treacherous thing. It lifts your soul to a height and then watches it descend. I have heard the song of this city. It is over now as I bend over a small shrub in the dark. It is unusually cold, and everything is quiet. I am in a sad place.

A little boy walks toward me. I try to remain calm, but the closer he gets, the more I sink to the earth.

"I saw you from a distance," says the boy. "I had to come."

He is made only of light. This boy is pure light.

"Can I help you?" he asks.

"Help. Why, I know what that is," I answer.

"Do you need it?"

"Yes," I say.

He puts his arms around me. I stand extremely still.

"Look at you," he says. "You are still entangled in your own embrace."

I look at myself. I do not have any arms to entangle myself in.

"Put your arms around me," he says. "Even if you have none."

I lean against his warm body. I close my eyes and send myself outward, without shame, until I know I am embracing him. I feel so much love that I might burst if this continues. He senses this and breaks away from me.

"Do you know I can fly?" he asks.

I remain quiet. I do not wish to dispute light.

"What am I thinking of right now?"

"Of flying?"

"Of flying, of tigers, of flying tigers."

I have heard these words before, a very long time ago. I remember seeing a warm, gold light above my head. I think back, very far back, to when I was at this same spot. As I look at this boy, I know what his next words will be. But I still wait for him to speak them.

"This place," he says. "It is very strange. There is magic, poverty, thievery, music, pollution, dancing, murder and lust."

"Yes," I say. "But this time there will also be prayer."

"What is this place called?" he asks.

"Bombay," I say.

"There is no other like it," he says.

ACKNOWLEDGMENTS

First of all, I am grateful to God, the Bhavnagris (especially Khorshed Aunty), my parents and Shiamak. I would like to thank George McWhirter for his guidance and encouragement throughout the writing of this book; my editor, Lynn Henry, for making suggestions with insight and thoughtfulness; and my agent, Denise Bukowski, for believing in my writing. Finally, a special thank you to Antonia Fusco and Elisabeth Scharlatt for all their support.